Zachariah Atwell Mudge

Foot Prints of Roger Williams

A Biography

Zachariah Atwell Mudge

Foot Prints of Roger Williams
A Biography

ISBN/EAN: 9783337252892

Printed in Europe, USA, Canada, Australia, Japan

Cover: Foto ©Raphael Reischuk / pixelio.de

More available books at **www.hansebooks.com**

FOOT-PRINTS

OF

ROGER WILLIAMS:

A Biography,

WITH

SKETCHES OF IMPORTANT EVENTS IN EARLY NEW
ENGLAND HISTORY, WITH WHICH HE
WAS CONNECTED.

By Rev. Z. A. MUDGE,

AUTHOR OF "WITCH HILL," "VIEWS FROM PLYMOUTH ROCK," "CHRISTIAN
STATESMAN," ETC.

FIVE ILLUSTRATIONS.

New York:
CARLTON & LANAHAN.
SAN FRANCISCO: E. THOMAS.
CINCINNATI: HITCHCOCK & WALDEN.
SUNDAY-SCHOOL DEPARTMENT.

PREFACE.

A MEMOIR of Roger Williams by Prof. J. D. Knowles was published in 1834. It contains all the material which was to be found at that time, and is a repository of knowledge to which all future writers on the subject must be greatly indebted. In 1846 Prof. William Gammel sent forth a Life of Roger Williams, and in 1853 Dr. Romeo Elton followed with another, both of which are interesting portraitures of his character. But none of these are professedly written for young people, for whom especially this volume is prepared.

Since the last date Samuel Greene Arnold has given to the public A History of Rhode Island and Providence Plantations. The work contains new facts concerning Williams, corrects some earlier investigations, and gives lucid statements of contemporaneous history with which he was connected.

Still later than this standard work has been the publication, by the Massachusetts Historical Society, of several letters written by Williams, which illustrate important periods of his life.

We have laid the above works under careful contribution in preparing our Foot-prints : besides these we are indebted for our sketches to Dr. Palfrey's History of New England, and to Drake's Biography and History of the North American Indians We have also introduced the rendering by the poets of a few of the facts of our narrative

We desire that our Foot-prints may inspire in the young a wish for a farther acquaintance with the thrilling events and noble characters of early American history, and that history may have for them a greater charm than fiction.

Our illustrations have never before been published in this connection, and will be found valuable.

CONTENTS.

CHAPTER IV.

WILLIAMS AT PLYMOUTH.

CHAPTER V.

AMONG OLD FRIENDS.

CHAPTER VI.

IN PERILS AMONG BRETHREN.

CHAPTER VII.

MORE PERILS.

CHAPTER VIII.

CAST OUT.

CHAPTER IX.

A STATE PLANTED.

CHAPTER X.

FRIENDLY GREETINGS TO MASSACHUSETTS.

CHAPTER XI.

INDIAN NEIGHBORS.

CHAPTER XII.

THE WAR-CLOUD.

CHAPTER XIII.

THE WAR-TEMPEST.

CHAPTER XIV.

AFTER THE STORM.

CHAPTER XV.

A BREEZE FROM ANOTHER QUARTER.

CHAPTER XVI.

FRIENDLY AID GIVEN.

CHAPTER XVII.

IMPORTANT CHANGES.

CHAPTER XVIII.

SOME SAD THINGS.

CHAPTER XIX.

MUCH PLEASANTER MATTERS.

CHAPTER XX.

AN OUT-LOOK FROM A TRADING-HOUSE.

CHAPTER XXI.

IN LONDON, WATCHING AND WAITING.

CHAPTER XXII.

WILLIAMS COLONIAL PRESIDENT.

CHAPTER XXIII.

A TERRIBLE COLLISION.

CHAPTER XXIV.

VARIOUS MATTERS.

CHAPTER XXV.

THE WAR-PATH.

CHAPTER XXVI.

THE SUNSET OF LIFE.

CHAPTER XXVII.

MEMENTOES.

Illustrations.

FOOT-PRINTS

OF

ROGER WILLIAMS.

————•◆•————

CHAPTER I.

THE FATHER-LAND.

THERE is an agreement, among critical inquirers, that Roger Williams was a Welshman. But the place and time of his birth have been in perplexing dispute. His first American biographer, a careful inquirer, settled upon 1599 as the year. He was followed at a later time by a learned investigator, who found the name of Roger Williams, as he supposed, in the records of Oxford University. It was written, as was the custom, in Latin, and read "Rodericus Williams." The year of his birth was given as 1606, and the place Conwyl Cayo, South Wales. We were right glad of this discovery, and were about to start, by the aid of some rare English volumes describing minutely the parishes of South Wales, to look up the foot-prints there of Roger Williams for the entertainment of our readers. But we felt, through a still later volume by a cautious and painstaking antiquary, a hand laid upon our shoulder. Look here, it was said; you had better not go to Cayo to look up localities connected with the early life of Roger Williams. "Rodericus" should not be rendered Roger, but Roderick, and so the record refers to quite another person. We felt a little mortified that we did not see the error for ourselves. This later author finds in the records of Pembroke College, Cambridge University, "Rogerus Williams," under a date which throws the time of his birth back to the year fixed upon by early writers, that of 1599. This, taken in connection with facts gathered from other sources, seems to settle the question of his age and place of classical training. His name was enrolled on the "admission book" of the University in 1623, and he took his degree of Bachelor of Arts in 1627. There is in connection with these dates his autograph signature, which, compared with his known signatures in this and the old country, shows that the records refer to *our* Roger Williams. He prepared for college at Sutton's Hospital, now the Charter House, where, about a hundred years later, John Wesley received his early training.

Williams was graded in the University as a Pensioner. All who boarded at the college were so classed. The sons of the noble and wealthy made a higher class, called Fellow Commoners. The poor students were arranged by themselves, and were called Sizars.

Roger Williams must have ranked well as a scholar in college, but very likely he was not popular among the students. He was too independent and out-spoken for general popularity, but could not have failed to make warm friends. He secured, as the records show, one of the under-graduate honors.

Though we do not know the place of his birth nor the names of his parents, we have, through some letters recently found, a pleasing incident of his early life, which largely determined the character and position of his whole future course. It also gives us a key to the spirit of his boyhood. At quite an early age he became accustomed to take notes of the sermons to which he listened. He also went to the court-rooms and took notes of the speeches. He was once taking notes in the Star Chamber, a famous criminal court of that day. An eminent lawyer, Sir Edward Coke—Lord Coke—noticed the boy thus employed, and, no doubt, was impressed with his promising appearance, for he examined his notes. The incident led to an acquaintance, and the acquaintance to the patronage of his lordship, who gave him his classical education.

Thus we find Roger Williams in 1627, at twenty-eight years of age, with college culture, launching into active life. His education was of course valuable at this important period, but he had that with it which was of priceless worth; he possessed an established religious character. He says of himself: "From my childhood the Father of lights and mercies touched my soul with a love to himself, to his only begotten the true Lord Jesus, and to his Holy Scriptures."

On leaving college he studied law for a while, probably through the prompting of Lord Coke, his patron. But the law was not his calling, so he soon turned to the ministry, and was ordained in the Episcopal Church. It is thought that he had for a short period a pastoral charge. Such was the state of England at this time that a man like Williams would not be allowed to remain long over a parish. His spirit was too independent. The opposing influence to such men was creating a commotion in the nation which was shaking it to its foundation. It was forming men's characters and shaping their destinies. It drove Williams to the New World, and was the spring of much of his future thought and action. But for this opposition he might have lived in an obscure parish, and died unknown to history. To fully appreciate, then, our story we must glance at the cause of this state of things.

During Williams' childhood Queen Elizabeth reigned in England, and had done so for many years. Her father, Henry VIII., had declared his independence of the Pope, but became a pope in spirit himself. Her sister Mary, a bigoted Roman Catholic, had during her short reign tortured and burned thousands of her Protestant subjects. Elizabeth was a Protestant by profession, and a tyrant in the exercise of her royal authority. Soon after her ascen-

sion to the throne she was declared the supreme
.head of the Church in her dominions. A law
was made about the same time, requiring uniformity not only of belief, but of the *manner* of
worship. A court was formed, called the Court
of High Commission, whose duty it was to see
that all the Queen's subjects submitted to her
supremacy in religion, and to uniformity in
worship. Of course no people of spirit, like
Englishmen, would submit quietly to such rulers
as Henry VIII., and his daughters Mary and
Elizabeth. A class of men grew up in these
reigns called by their enemies *Puritans*, in de-
rision of their efforts to secure a purer religious
faith and practice. But it was not a bad name.
They of course increased in numbers and
strength the more they were persecuted. The
following incident will show how the Puritan
ministers were treated by the High Commission
Court—the Protestant Inquisition. Its officer
cited, at one time, the London clergy before
him. He set before them a minister of his own
sort, dressed in a square cap, a priest-like scholar's gown, and a tippet. They were told they
must dress like this man, and wear a linen sur-
plice in the pulpit. " Now," said the officer to

them, " ye that will submit to this order of apparel, write *volo;* ye that will not submit, write *nolo.* Be brief, make no words!" Those who did not submit were turned out of their parishes, and often left with their families in great destitution. This course of oppression left only two thousand ministers to serve ten thousand churches.

Such was the state of things in Williams' childhood. From that time, 1603, until his second year in college, 1625, James I. reigned. The state of the nation grew worse and worse. The King's understanding was very weak, but he thought it wonderfully strong ; he was ignorant, but thought himself learned ; he was wicked in heart and life, but by persecuting those who did not believe as he did he persuaded himself that he was very pious. One of his strong passions was a love of flattery, and, of course, as he had royal favors to bestow, his courtiers gave him all of it he wanted. They called him the British Solomon. The Duke of Sully said more truthfully: "King James is the wisest fool in Europe." Bishop Burnet added, "He is the scorn of the age!"

Think of Englishmen being quiet under such

a ruler, with all the laws of "supremacy" and "conformity" enforced! They became about as much so as autumn leaves in a whirlwind.

There was one good thing done in the reign of James. The Bible was given to the world in the translation in which we now read it. God had the King in hand when this was done, making his stupidity and wickedness to praise him. Men began more than ever to read the pure word, and so more and more hated the rulers and laws which restrained their consciences.

Charles I. began to reign in 1625. He was a wiser man than his foolish father, but not a wise ruler. He was playing the despot with his people, when, in the latter part of 1630, Williams was preparing to leave the country. His native air was tainted by this spirit of oppression, and the stormy atmosphere of New England would be to him as the breath of Eden if it but sustained the spirit of civil and religious liberty. We shall see how well his hopes in this respect were realized.

CHAPTER II.

ACROSS THE SEA.

WE have seen the burdens which rested upon the free spirit of Roger Williams in the Father-land. What was there, as he looked across the sea to the New World, to inspire his hope of a land more free, and a home more quiet? Let us look at it for a moment through his eyes.

The older settlements south of New England did not encourage his coming to their territory. They were too much in sympathy with the King and the Church party.

He would look, therefore, farther north. He must have known well the history of that devoted band of Christians which left England when he was only seven years of age. Their tarrying in Holland fourteen years, and their subsequent perilous voyage to America ten years before this, must have been subjects of study with him in his early manhood. Theirs was an experience which suited his turn of mind.

Their struggles at Plymouth, fighting with cold, poverty, sickness, and savage foes, all for a purer worship, was perhaps the inspiration of his present purpose to cross the sea.

But just now a company of men were making a settlement not far from the Plymouth Pilgrims, which promised a wider field of labor for a Christian minister. So to them the attention of Williams was attracted. It was the Massachusetts colony. King James had granted a magnificent right in the New World to the Plymouth Company, made up of rich merchants and powerful noblemen. By this they were made owners of the country between the fortieth and forty-eighth degrees of north latitudes, from the Atlantic to the Pacific Ocean. Let the reader take the map and see if this does not look like a grand landed estate. It included a large part of what is now the dominion of Canada, all of New England and New York, large portions of Pennsylvania, New Jersey, Ohio, Indiana, and Illinois, all of the great States of Michigan, Wisconsin, Iowa, and Minnesota, and the vast area of the States and Territories west of these, across the Rocky Mountains to the Pacific Ocean. But great possessions are not

always great riches.   This huge farm proved to
be an unmanageable elephant to its owners, and
they returned to the King soon after their title-
deed with a " Thank you, sir ; we don't care for
it any longer."

Of this Company some wealthy men, called
the Massachusetts Bay Company, obtained a
patent, March 14, 1628, to so much of their territory as lay between lines drawn from the
Atlantic Ocean to the Pacific, starting three
miles north of the Merrimac river, and three
miles south of the Charles river.   The new
Company sent over the same year a party under
John Endicott, who began a settlement at Salem.   They found a few adventurers there, the
most of whom left at their coming.   The next
year, 1629, the Rev. Francis Higginson headed
a company of two hundred persons, who sought
homes at Salem and Charlestown.   In 1630 an
expedition of eight hundred persons came over,
with John Winthrop as Governor.   During the
year nearly as many more followed, all settling
in and about Boston and Charlestown.   Endicott gracefully yielded his official position to
Winthrop, and the career of the Massachusetts
colony was fully begun.   The King had granted

them, by charter, full power to make all necessary laws "not repugnant to England." They
were to give his Majesty one fifth of all the gold
and silver ores which they found in the country.
Neither party became rich on these.

These men had largely in view mercantile
advantages. But many of them, including
most of the leading men, had higher aims.
They sought to establish a government which
should not only allow but enforce a religious
faith and worship which agreed with their own
convictions of what God required. We wish
we could say that they sought to erect a State
allowing all to serve God as they believed he
commanded, leaving them to give account in
this matter to him alone.

But so earnest were they to promote the religious interest of the people that the first law
they made was designed to secure the support
of their ministers. The second one related to
the arrest of a man by the name of Morton,
who was having a good time generally at Merry
Mount, in what is now Quincy. They thus
sought to secure for the State a sound faith and
a correct behavior.

These emigrants to Salem, Charlestown,

Boston, and vicinity, had severe disciplining
during their early months in the country.
Though no Indians lurked behind the rocks and
trees to dispute their landing, a more relentless foe awaited them.   When Winthrop arrived
at Salem eighty had died, their provisions were
becoming alarmingly scanty, and their distress
was very great.   Soon after the Governor's
company and those who immediately succeeded
them had become settled, two hundred were cut
down by death.   Pestilence and famine challenged their right to the land.   Consternation
seized upon them, and a hundred returned home
before the close of the first year, carrying with
them discouragement to their friends in England.   The emigration consequently went on
slowly, and the next two years scarcely made up
the losses.

While in the early part of 1631 the colonists
were in the midst of their sore distress from
sickness and famine, news was brought that a
ship lay off Nantasket.   It proved to be the
good ship Lyon, Captain William Peirce, with
twenty passengers, and a large quantity of provisions.   The good news revived every drooping heart.   A fast was to have been observed, by

official appointment, on the day after that of the arrival. The mourning had been turned into joy, and, instead, a day of thanksgiving was observed.

This ship, which sent a thrill of gladness throughout the colony, brought Roger Williams and his wife Mary. In defiance of the difficulties to be encountered, the essential character of which must have been known to them, they had turned their backs on the oppression of the Old World. The circumstances of their arrival doubtless made the welcome from their brethren all the more cordial. What perils awaited him among those brethren were wisely hid in the future, but were soon developed.

CHAPTER III.

GETTING ACQUAINTED.

MR. WILLIAMS was now in Boston. Not, of course, the Boston of to-day. He stepped ashore from a small colony ship, glad to escape from the narrow, crowded cabin after a stormy passage of about nine weeks. Men land now from the palace-like accommodations of ocean steamers after a trip of ten or twelve days. Three wood-covered hills, within whose coverts the wild animals were unmolested, greeted his view. Now one of those hills has been leveled, the other two have lost much of their prominence, and the marshy intervals have been filled. Winthrop's company, who had been on the site but a few months, had put up a few huts and pitched a few tents. Probably these were scattered about the forest, so as not all to be seen at once. Now the State-House crowning one of the hills, the numerous church spires, the massive public buildings, the dwelling houses densely crowded together, and the almost countless multitudes which throng the streets, or which fly in and out on the steam cars, evince time's mighty changes.

Now Boston is full of luxuries. The following is an early historian's picture of its want and misery when Williams arrived: "The weather held tolerable until the 24th of December, but the cold then came on with violence. Such a Christmas eve they had never seen before. From that time to the 10th of February their chief care was to keep themselves warm, and as comfortable in other respects as their scanty provisions would permit. The poorer sort were much exposed, lying in tents and miserable hovels, and many died of the scurvy and other distempers. They were so short of provisions that many were obliged to live upon clams, muscles, and other shell-fish, with ground nuts and acorns instead of bread. One who came to the Governor's house to complain of his sufferings was prevented, being informed that even there the last batch was in the oven. Some instances are mentioned of great calmness and resignation in this distress. One man who asked his neighbor to a dish of clams, after dinner returned thanks to God who had given them to suck of the abundance of the seas, and treasures hid in the sands."

Winthrop found one white man on the peninsula of " Trimountain." His name was William Blackstone, a clergyman from England. He hospitably invited the new-comers to occupy the locality with him, pointing them, as an inducement, to its sweet springs of water. Would that Boston now had only *sweet springs*, and that all the fountains from which its people drink were as health-giving as its first settler's pure water! Blackstone soon gave the cold shoulder to his invited guests. He declared that he left England because he disliked the Lords Bishops, and he liked as little the Lord's Brethren. He was hard to please. He seemed to like his own company, for he moved to a lonely cabin in the Indian country near the Narragansett Bay. The river on the banks of which he settled now bears his name. It has generally been stated that he was the first settler within the present limits of Rhode Island. But he did not go there until 1638, so this honor belongs to Roger Williams.*

* Letter of Samuel G. Drake in the N. E. Historical and Genealogical Magazine of October, 1861.

Though Williams found so little else when he
arrived in Boston, he found an organized Church
having a Pastor.   Arrangements for it had been
made on shipboard, and carried out by Governor Winthrop and others as soon as they
landed at Charlestown.   It had, of course, come
with them to the peninsula.   Their Church
covenant was very simple.   They said: "We
promise to walk in all our ways according to
the rule of the Gospel, and in all sincere conformity to God's holy ordinances, and in mutual
love and respect to each other, so near as he
shall give us grace."   Mr. Wilson was elected
"teacher" or Pastor.   They laid their hands
upon his head as do the Bishops in ministerial
ordination in the Episcopal Church.   "But," says
Winthrop, "with this protestation by all, that it
was only as a sign of election and confirmation,
not of any intent that Mr. Wilson should re-
nounce his ministry that he received in England."

This Church had no house of worship at this
time, but erected one the next year.   It was a
humble structure, with thatched roof, and walls
whose crevices were stopped with mud.   Its
vocal prayers, we doubt not, were as acceptable
to its Divine Head as if they echoed from the

walls of a house costing, as many in Boston do now, a hundred thousand dollars ; and its songs needed not, for the securement of his favor, the swelling, mighty tones of the great organ in its Music Hall. It was situated on the south side of State-street, near where princely merchants and bustling business men now congregate " on 'change."

This Church promptly and unanimously elected Williams teacher.* This was making him essentially an associate Pastor. But "upon examination and conference," finding them "an unseparated people," he declined what must otherwise have been to him an exceedingly desirable position. By "an unseparated people," we understand that he meant a people too much sympathizing with and fellowshiping the Church of England.

Williams remained in Boston only a few weeks. He received a call from brethren in Salem, which he gladly accepted, as already it had become apparent that he could not see "eye to eye" with the principal men of Boston.

It would be curious enough if we could follow him and his wife in their removal to Salem.

* Proceedings of Mass. His. Soc. 1855–1858, pp. 313–316.

It is quite probable that they journeyed on horseback, perhaps on one horse.   After crossing
the Charles river, they slowly picked their way
along an Indian trail, through what is now
Charlestown, near Bunker Hill, through Somer-
ville, Malden, and Lynn, fording the streams,
making quite a circuit at times to avoid boggy
swamps or precipitous rocks, arriving at Salem
at nightfall, after a long and weary day's journey.   If they had waited until our day before
taking their journey they would have stepped
into the Eastern Depot, taken the "lightning
train," heard the conductor say "All aboard,"
chatted about half an hour, and then left at the
call, "Salem."

The hearts of the tired travelers were made
glad, we have no doubt, when they reached their
stopping-place.   Ex-Governor Endicott, who
had been there almost three years, had a Governor's house to which to invite them, and, what
was better, had a generous and warm heart with
which he cheered them.   His Pastor, the Rev.
Mr. Skelton, bade them welcome.   A goodly
settlement contrasted cheerfully with the rough
beginning at Boston.   The Rev. Francis Higginson, who had brought with him about two

years before a company of two hundred persons, had just died. He was an eloquent
preacher, a ripe scholar, and an eminent Christian. The tears were still moistening the faces
of his bereaved flock. Higginson on his arrival
had found "about halfe a score of houses, and
a faire house newly built for the Governour;"
and he added, in his account sent to London:
"We found abundance of corn planted by them,
very good and well liking." It was too early in
the season for Williams to be cheered by the
sight of corn, even in the blade, and looking at
the soil, mostly sandy, he perhaps wondered
how any thing ever grew in it. The town was
situated on a neck of land made by two arms
of the sea, called the North and South rivers.
Looking seaward, his soul must have been
stirred by the beautiful and grand scenery.
The varied and rocky shore line presented a
defiant barrier to the sea, whose waves, as they
dashed against it, rolled back in angry foam, or
floated away in misty clouds. The bay, as far
as the eye could reach, was studded with numerous islands, some of which lifted their craggy
heads as the sullen custodians of the coast,
while others smiled with springing verdure, pre-

paring a summer greenness to welcome the coming, ocean-weary emigrants. Inland was an almost unbroken forest which a man of more lively imagination might have peopled with lurking savages and ferocious beasts, and which the misinformed Higginson did make the hiding place of prowling lions. A little later in the season Williams saw the unpromising soil about the settlement bearing a bountiful crop of all necessary produce under the prompting "of a fishing once in three years," after the Indian fashion.

With these goodly surroundings, the company of Christian friends, and a call from the people to make up, as far as possible, the loss of their late "teacher," by becoming an assistant to Mr. Skelton, Mr. Williams and his wife must have felt that their lines had fallen in a pleasant place.

The people of Salem, like those of Boston, had been prompt in providing the means of supporting a minister. Soon after the arrival of Mr. Higginson, thirty persons entered into a written covenant in the formation of a Church. Its terms were very liberal, and its statements simple. The Puritan Churches of those days considered two ministers necessary to the complete instruction of their people. They did not differ much in their duties, and answered pretty well to the senior and junior Pastors of the present day. They had also Ruling Elders and Deacons, having a general relation to the official character of Deacons in the Congregational Churches now.

The Salem Church ordained, after the manner of Winthrop's people, Mr. Skelton, Pastor, and Mr. Higginson, teacher.

This new Church in the wilderness, having a vivid remembrance of the oppression they suffered in the. Old World from their spiritual rulers, were very jealous of their rights. They invited Governor Bradford and some of his brethren of the Plymouth Pilgrim Church to come and take a part in the ceremony. But before these guests were permitted to give the right hand of fellowship they were required to disclaim obtaining by this act any right of interference or control. The Pilgrims might have smiled at such caution, but probably their own experience had taught them to think it was all right.

Thus in seeming peace was this infant Church cradled, with no frowning King to thunder against it, nor agent of the Lord Bishop to say, "Conform; be brief; no words." But a cloud appeared in their sunny sky. Several influential men, the leaders of whom were John and Samuel Brown, thought a *reform* of the ceremonies of worship in the father-land the desirable course, and disapproved of the present entire rejection of them. So they set up a separate place of worship, and used in their congregation the book of common prayer. But, as we have stated, our Puritan fathers sought this far-off land, and submitted to its self-denials, to form a Church and State after *their* pattern. Those wishing a different one should, they insisted, seek for themselves a nook where they could do the same. So the gentlemen brothers Brown were informed that they had leave to return to England. They understood that this hint meant, Go! and they went. Their brethren of like faith subsided into conformity.

This cloud had scarcely been dissipated from the sky of the Salem Church when Roger Williams came, and new difficulties sprang up. Now their call for his services caused a muttering thunder from a cloud dark and threatening, rising in the direction of Boston. The brethren

there did not like some items of the proposed
Pastor's faith. He had told them that they
ought to repent of their fault in having had
communion with the Churches in England. He
even refused · to join in their public worship,
because they did not make a public declaration
of such repentance. He had further declared
to them that in his opinion the Courts should
not punish violations of the first four of the ten
commandments, because they contained require-
ments which concerned not the State, but men's
consciences only, and so were to be left to them
and God.

The Court at Boston wrote to ex-Governor
Endicott, of Salem, that, in view of these sentiments avowed by Williams, they were surprised they should choose him without consult-
ing them.

On the very day that this letter of the Court
was written, the Salem people, fully aware of the
objections it expressed, settled Williams as their
minister.

Every person now will say that the Salem
Church was right. Why need rulers fifteen
miles away concern themselves about the Salem
society's matters? But we shall further see

that the interference of the authorities was consistent with the notions of the Puritan Churches
of that day concerning right and duty.

As to the matters of difference between Williams and the Boston ministers, and precisely
what was done or believed which caused the
coldness, we do not know. But so far as we
can understand them, as set forth in the letter
of the Court, they were small occasions indeed
for the separation of brethren. Why could they
not "think and let think?" Some believe that
jealousy of Salem on the part of Boston was
in part the secret spring of this interference,
for Salem aspired at this time to be the capital
of the colony. But we prefer to believe only
what the Court avowed.

The settlement of Williams at Salem occurred
in April, 1631, and before the year closed the
troubles made his place uncomfortable, and he
sought a quiet refuge by a removal to the more
liberal Pilgrims at Plymouth.

CHAPTER IV.

WILLIAMS AT PLYMOUTH.

FROM Salem to Plymouth must have been, to Mr. Williams and his family, in many respects a pleasant change. The Pilgrims had been eleven years in the country, toiling dili⸱ gently to improve their homes ; but the Salem settlement, as we have seen, was only three years old. True, the Bay Colony had more money to expend in family conveniences, yet we think that Williams and his wife found more at Plymouth to remind them of the father-land than they had found since coming to America. From the shore where the Pilgrims had landed to the hill immediately inland they had already quite a busy, populous street. Dwellings, with enclosed lots and cultivated gardens, lined each side of it. Their store-house was near the shore end of the street, and at the other end, on the top of the hill, was their " block-house," bristling with cannon, of no very formidable character as things go now, but terrific, no doubt, to their Indian foes. The whole settlement was inclosed with a stockade, and the military genius of Captain Standish had given quite a warlike aspect to this Christian encampment. This would not, we think, strike the pacific spirit of their guest favorably, though he must have seen its justification in their peculiar situation.

Once domiciled among the Pilgrims, a man of cultivated mind and Christian heart like Williams could not fail to like them. Until a house could be built for him he would be likely to live with their Pastor, Ralph Smith, or with their Elder, William Brewster ; perhaps they all, for the time, made one family. Whether this was so or not, these three religious teachers, and Standish the soldier, and Bradford and Winslow, the civil rulers, must have been often together—a goodly company. All except Smith possessed sharp lines of character, all were students and thinkers, and every one felt the pressure of the stirring times in which they lived, and the perils of the position in which they were placed. What earnest discussions there must have been ! What serious debates must have occurred in that little company concerning weighty matters of Church and State !

In expounding great principles, wisely applicable to all men and all ages, Williams was the prince of the group. But these good men would not always in their fireside meetings be talking of theories. They were practical men, and their positions demanded work. They were all much concerned—perhaps we ought to except the soldier—in the great matter of holy living, When this theme was the subject of conversation, as it would be often, none could speak more wisely than the devout Brewster. We think they all listened willingly and with great profit to his luminous expositions of God's word, which he read in the original languages, and to the results of his long experience of the saving power and rich comforts of the grace of God. When questions of defense against the savages were in debate, it was Standish's turn to be chief adviser ; and when the weighty business concerns of the colony came up for friendly counsel, the sound judgment of Bradford, and, more especially, the comprehensive business mind of Winslow, were brought into prominence. Thus in turn they were teachers and learners, and thus they strengthened each other's hands and hearts.

This group at the Pilgrim fireside, with its additions from time to time, had its social chats in which matters of personal interest were related—incidents of trials and triumphs which increased the bond of affection between relater and hearers. If the author had been there he could have written, no doubt, several additional chapters, which now must be forever unwritten, concerning Mr. Williams' previous history. Though debarred from this privilege, we are safe in reporting some of the talk of the Mayflower men, and, as we are to accompany Williams in his stay with them during about two years, we shall be well entertained by the principal facts concerning their previous eleven years at Plymouth.

The sickness of the Pilgrims just after their landing was a subject of sad conversation. One half of their number died, among whom was Carver, their Governor. All the survivors except seven were prostrate with disease at one time. Bradford often held Williams' willing ears in rehearsing the incidents of those anxious days when Brewster and Standish, two of the favored seven, with a true Christian devotion, spared not themselves in unpleasant

drudgery or exposure to relieve their suffering brethren. Brewster's turn came to lead the
conversation, when the incidents of the third
summer were topics of conversation. The terrible drought which reduced them to a very
scanty allowance of food, making " treasures in
the sand " a luxury, was glowingly depicted.
The fast which it occasioned, the personal hu-
miliations, the confessions of private and public
sins, and the earnest supplication for Divine
help, were related with deep feeling. But
Brewster dwelt with devout gratitude, shared by
all his listening friends, upon the gracious answers to these prayers—the coming of the
" soft, sweet, and joyous showers," reviving not
only the parched fields, but their "drooping
graces." Then followed a glad account of the
harvest which was gathered in the fall and the
consequent Thanksgiving day—the mother of
all " Thanksgiving days," which have extended
from ocean to ocean, and from Canada to the
Gulf of Mexico, causing the yearly repetition
of the Pilgrim story in almost every home of
our wide extended country. .

Bradford has left in his journal evidence of
his taste for treasuring up the incidents of the

daily life of the Pilgrims.   So we think he would
tell the stories of their explorations about Cape
Cod, and in the vicinity of what is now Charlestown and Boston, to ascertain the temper of
their Indian neighbors, but more especially to
trade with them for furs and corn.   He did
not forget their many early *scares* about the Indians, at which the group could afford to laugh.
But the fact of the final coming of the Chief
Massasoit and his warriors, their treaty with
him, and his faithful performance thus far of its
conditions, was dwelt upon with gratitude to
God.

When Standish was prominent in the talk, he
must have referred to a plot by a bold, low-
minded savage to cut off by Indian butchery a
new colony near Plymouth, and to include afterward the Pilgrims in the ruin.   But we do not
think he dwelt in detail upon his hand to hand
fight with the conspirator Wituwamat, and his
taking his head off, and bringing it to Plymouth,
and placing it at the gate of their defenses to
intimidate their enemies.   Such sad affairs the
Pilgrims felt to be an imposed necessity which
they would willingly forget.   Very likely when
this incident was talked about that Williams

in his outspoken way called in question the necessity of the harsh measure to secure safety ; but we think the Pilgrims made a good case in their own defense.

The Pilgrims at the time Williams went among them were burdened with a heavy debt, incurred in the expense of transporting themselves and friends to the New World. It greatly afflicted them not only before but for many years after this time. Winslow and Standish had at different times returned to England in reference to it. Allerton, one of the Mayflower men, had been there a long time as their confidential agent, and had so mismanaged as to increase their debt, and had just been dismissed from their service, if not in disgrace, with feelings of great dissatisfaction toward him. This was a painful theme of talk, and we doubt whether Mr. Williams could give the Pilgrims any advice concerning these matters worth taking. It is certain that he never managed financial matters well for himself, though for others he sometimes did better.

On Mr. Williams' arrival at Plymouth he was made by the Plymouth Church assistant Pastor, without the fear of the Boston authorities before their eyes. The principal Pastor, Ralph Smith, had a few years before been found in distress at Nantasket. John Robinson, their Pastor in Holland, with whom they had hoped to be re-united in the New World, had died in 1625—about seven years before. Before Smith's arrival they had made two efforts to secure a Pastor. The first, after a vexatious trial, proved to them by his conduct that he had never known the divine remedy for a diseased heart. The second, an estimable young man, was afflicted with a disease of the brain, and was soon returned to England. But covering the whole time which they had been without a Pastor, Brewster, their Elder, had, without the name and formality of a preacher, been to them a God-approved teacher of religion.

Leaving the Pilgrims for a short time to become better acquainted with their assistant Pastor before we inquire how they liked him, we will more narrowly observe the manner in which Williams employs his time at Plymouth. We are prepared to learn that he is seeking to do good, but may be surprised at the method he adopts to secure that end. He is leaving the comfortable home and good company of the

Pilgrims and his own wife, and is spending much of his time in the disgusting wigwams and disagreeable society of the heathen Indians. His object is to learn their language, that he may impart to them a knowledge of the Saviour of men, and lead them through him from sin to holiness, and so from earth to heaven. The end sought is worthy of his Christian heart, and of the time and self-sacrificing toil it will require. This noble enterprise has been prompted, we think, by what he has learned concerning Massasoit and his people. Winslow has spent several days and nights with his savage Majesty, and has given Williams all the details of court manners and style of living. So Williams knows what price he is to pay for the privilege of speaking of Jesus to the savages. Some of these details given in reference to Winslow's first visit to the King will show in part what that price is. The first night the visitor went to bed supperless, not for lack of hospitality, but because of the destitution of food at head-quarters. He was permitted, however, to share the royal couch, which was made of planks with a single mat thrown over them. The Queen slept across the foot of the same bed. Swarms of vermin, added to weariness, cold, and hunger, drove sleep from the Pilgrim. The Indians soothed themselves to sleep by a dismal chanting, to which the musquitoes added their buzzing lullaby. Such was the night. During the day his eyes were offended by the constant sight of greasy, painted, half-naked men and women, and at all times his nostrils assailed by "offensive and poisonous odors."

With such human beings in such abodes, Williams joyfully spent much of the time of his Plymouth pastorate.

Turning to Plymouth, we are able to look in upon their Sabbath worship, and see the part that Williams takes in it.

In September, 1632, Roger Williams having been in Plymouth a year, Governor Winthrop, of Massachusetts, his warm, steadfast Christian friend, and stern official opponent, made that place a visit. His Pastor, Mr. Wilson, and others accompanied him. The party landed from a vessel at what is now North Weymouth, and walked from thence to Plymouth. Governor Bradford and his officials met them out of town, and escorted them in. Rulers in those days magnified their office with due ceremony. The visitors were feasted at the Governor's house. When the Sabbath came the whole company went to Church. The block-house audience of stern men, resolute but kindly looking women, and hardy children, had never worn a pleasanter aspect. A few Indians were doubtless attentive listeners to the service, among whom Hobomok, the tried friend of the Pilgrims, was conspicuous. In the morning was administered the sacrament of the Lord's Supper, of which they all partook, Williams having wisely laid aside some of the scruples which so offended his friends at Boston. In the afternoon they were again at the house of God. According to their custom, Williams "propounded a question"—which means, we suppose, a question founded upon some cited text of Scripture. The Pastor, Mr. Smith, spoke upon this question. He was followed by Mr. Williams, Governor Bradford, Elder Brewster, and several of the congregation, all keeping to the question. Then, on invitation, Governor Winthrop and Mr. Wilson spoke upon it. After this, Deacon Fuller reminded the congregation of the duty of contribution. Then followed not the passing of the contribution box round, but the marching of the congregation to it at the Deacon's seat, depositing their gifts, and returning to their places.

This must have been a very enjoyable time. It prepares us for Bradford's declaration concerning Williams. Here it is: "He was freely entertained among us according to our poor ability. He exercised his gifts among us, and after some time was admitted a member of the Church. His preaching was well approved, for the benefit of which I shall bless God. I am thankful to him even for his sharpest admonitions and reproofs, so far as they agreed with truth."

Toward the close of his stay with the Pilgrims, an interesting incident occurred in Mr. Williams' domestic circle. It was the birth of his eldest daughter, who was named Mary, after her mother.

The time was now come for Mr. Williams to leave Plymouth. He had laid the foundation of a critical acquaintance with the Indian language, and, what was scarcely less valuable, inspired a confidence in his integrity and benevolence in the minds of leading sachems. The Church at Salem was fearing the rapid decline of Mr. Skelton's health, and invited Williams

to become his assistant. The majority of the
Pilgrims were reluctant to have him depart, so
warm had become their Christian attachment.
Elder Brewster, however, favored his dismissal.
Difference of opinion on grave matters had
been developed, it seems, between Williams and
some of the leading men. A small number of
the Pilgrim Church were so attached to Mr.
Williams that they obtained their dismissal at
the same time, and accompanied him to Salem.

His departure from Plymouth took place in
the latter part of August, 1633.

CHAPTER V.

AMONG OLD FRIENDS.

MR. WILLIAMS, with his wife and little Mary, found himself at once pleasantly situated, so far as his relations to the Church and community were concerned. Their renewed call shows that their first love was not abated. The senior Pastor, Mr. Skelton, whom in his declining health he came to assist, was a tried friend of kindred spirit. An incidental but important matter of consideration to the faithful shepherd was the generous provision made for his domestic comfort. When Francis Higginson arrived in 1629 he brought orders from the London Company to Governor Endicott to build for him a parsonage at the public expense. This was promptly done, and another was provided for Mr. Skelton. No doubt a comfortable one was provided for Mr. Williams. We suppose it was a humble house in size, architecture, and furnishing, but it was a Christian home, which gave it a beautiful adorning

Though the Society had two public instruct-
ors, it had no house of worship. An unfinished
building of one story was being temporarily
occupied. That important setting apart of
Skelton and Higginson for the ministry in 1629,
which we have noticed, probably took place in
this building, unless, it being midsummer, the
service took the form of a grove meeting, which
is not unlikely. What could be more appro-
priate than that the service connected with the
organization of the first Church ever gathered
in New England, and the first ministerial ordination, should be under the open canopy of heaven!
This and the Plymouth Church, a goodly plant
transferred at an earlier date to New England
soil, were then the only Churches.

It would be pleasant now, since Mr. Williams
is so comfortably situated among his flock, to
look into their inner Church life. No doubt
there were seasons of song and of prayer in the
"unfinished building" very precious to the
people of God. It must have been very cold
there in the winter season, and very likely they
were on stormy Sundays driven to some wealthy
brother's large kitchen, and around his cheer-
ful fire listened to the word preached. A

religious service in the evening was not, we presume, ever attempted.

There is a pleasant record by an old author, writing only five years later than Williams' coming to Salem, of the manner of receiving persons into the Church. This writer says that the applicants talked with the Pastors in private, who, if they were satisfied with the genuineness of their conversion, proposed them at the next public meeting, where the merits of their case might be discussed. It was common in the *Boston* Churches for the men only who were seeking admission to relate their experience in these general assemblies ; the Pastors reported for the women. But this old writer says : " At Salem the women speak for themselves, for the most part, in the Church ; but of late it is said they do this upon the week days there, and nothing is done on Sunday but their entrance into covenant."

This is an interesting fact that the first Puritan New England Church admitted at their public meetings the recital by the sisters of their Christian experience. Was this due to the broad views of Roger Williams concerning Christian duty and privilege ?

The next year after Williams' return to Salem the Society appropriated five hundred dollars for the building of a house of worship. A Mr. Norton took the contract for that purpose and at that sum. It was, when completed, twenty feet in length, seventeen in width, and twelve in the height of its posts. It had a gallery over the door at the entrance, and a minister's seat at the opposite side. The seats for the people were very rough if they were in keeping with the other parts of the building, probably split logs without backs.

We have no account of the dedicatory service. No doubt that on the occasion the people came from their already scattered homes in the immediate town and vicinity. The Pastor was full of thanksgiving and hope, and the people of joy. We may well believe that no later house built by their descendants, of splendid architectural beauty and costly furnishing, has been hailed with greater gladness. Mr. Williams was indeed among his friends.

CHAPTER VI.

IN PERILS AMONG BRETHREN.

OVER the pleasant pastoral field of Salem Williams soon saw the clouds gathering. They were at first very small, dark specks in the horizon—very trifling affairs certainly to be the hiding places of tempests so terrific as those which followed.

In the November following the return of Williams, certain " ministers' meetings " were pressed upon the notice of himself and colleague. They appear to have been gatherings of the Pastors of Boston, Charlestown, and Saugus, in turn at their parsonages, for mutual pleasure and profit. Mr. Skelton, smarting, as most of the Puritan clergymen had been made to smart, under the oppressive priestly rule of the old country, thought he saw a future " presbytery," or " superintendency," or some such monster breeding in these meetings. Like a faithful watchman, he blew the alarm in Zion. If it was a false alarm, it proved at least his watchful jealousy. Williams sympathized with his fears, but was not foremost in awakening the flock. When other charges were brought against him, this seems to have been remembered, and has since been urged to his disparagement.

There was another profound question of the times into which Williams is said to have been drawn, although there is no reliable evidence that he took a prominent part in its discussion. It was, "Shall the women wear vails in the religious assemblies?" We commend it to the consideration of the Freshmen of our colleges. This question was rife in the colony when Williams came to Salem, and Governor Endicott and his Pastor, Skelton, were committed to the affirmative side. At a lecture in Boston, while Williams was yet in Plymouth, Endicott and one of the greatest and best of the ministers, John Cotton, debated this question before the people. The disputants waxed so warm that the Governor, who presided, "perceiving it to grow to some earnestness," interposed and closed the meeting.

This trifling question too has been unjustly connected with Williams' name to his disparagement.

But more serious matters connected with Mr. Williams soon crowded these out of sight. While at Plymouth he wrote his views of certain political questions of no very vital importance, and presented them to the Governor and Council of that colony, which seem not to have disturbed the good feeling toward him among the Pilgrims, nor alarmed them in anywise. Now, Williams being in the Bay Colony, its Governor requires a copy of him, though the document had been written for the private satisfaction of the Plymouth authorities alone. His Excellency reads it and is alarmed. He and his Council consult the ministers, who, though not admitted as legal members of the government, are an ever ready and decisive power outside of it. They read Mr. Williams' treatise, and "much condemn his error and presumption." The Court then order that he should be "convented" at their next session—that is, brought before their honors " to be censured." The Governor wrote to Endicott, telling him what had been done, and requested him "to deal with" his heretical Pastor to secure his retraction of his document. Williams wisely added no fuel to this kindling fire, but answered the disturbed authorities in a conciliatory spirit. He even offered his manuscript, or any part of it, to be burnt. At the next Court he gave satisfaction as to his intention and loyalty, and the affair ended.

The reader would like to know what the opinions of Williams were which made such a stir. According to the statement of them by the Court they were: That King James told a solemn public lie when he said in his patent that he was the first Christian Prince who discovered New England ; that, further, the King was guilty of blasphemy in calling Europe Christendom or the Christian world ; and, still further, that he applied certain passages in Revelations to the reigning King, Charles. The Court does not say what passages they were.

We do not wonder that " the Council on further examination found the matters not to be so evil as they first seemed." To see any evil in them they doubtless looked through their fears of the home government.

This cloud having passed away, the Salem minister was allowed to pursue his official duties in peace for nearly a year. In August, 1634,

Mr. Skelton died. The Church soon invited the assistant to be ordained as a regular Pastor. The magistrates sent them their disapproval of such proposed ordination. The Church nevertheless proceeded and placed the man of their choice over them as "teacher." He had won the confidence of the professed Christians, and the people generally, as a true Christian, a faithful minister, and a man of ability.

In November of the same year Mr. Williams was again summoned before the Court. His sin consisted in persisting to talk against the King's patent, which he said could not give a good title to lands occupied by the Indians without a purchase from them. This the King claimed in the patent to do, though the colonies had not acted upon that claim, but satisfied the Indians. It would seem, then, that the authorities did not so much object to the opinion as the *talk* about it, especially the talk by Williams. They claimed that he promised to keep his tongue still on the matter, though we have no account of his understanding of the engagement.

From this time to the following April, 1635, there was a lull in the gathering storm of con-

tention. The court then met and cited Williams
before them on a new complaint. They certainly kept a tireless watch of their Salem
neighbor. This time: "The occasion was for
that he had taught publicly that a magistrate
ought not to tender an oath to an unregenerate
man, for that we thereby have communion with
a wicked man in the worship of God, and cause
him to take the name of God in vain."

Williams, it appears from some of his later
writings, had suffered financial loss in the English court from their imposition of oaths he
could not conscientiously take, and he had
there become impressed that the exacting of
oaths on trifling occasions caused men to treat
God's name lightly. From this he had come
to believe an oath a part of worship, and so improper for unrenewed men ; and as they were
improper for such to take, it was wrong for
courts to require them.

The penalty imposed upon Williams at this
time by the court for this opinion was a very
fitting one for Christian men to inflict and for
a good man to receive. They required him to
debate the matter before them with the ministers. He had his parishioner, Endicott, on his

side. Williams and Endicott were "very clear-
ly confuted," in the estimation of their opponents, and, as both sides usually triumph in
such cases, it must have proved a good time all
round.

But the debate about oaths proved not to be
the end of the affair. The magistrates being
alarmed about " some Episcopal and malignant
practices against the country," demanded of all
the freemen an oath of fidelity to the laws of
the colony. This was in addition to an oath
they had already taken to yield obedience to all
laws not in conflict with the laws of the mother
country. The new oath made the colony supreme. This new test of fidelity Mr. Williams
"vehemently withstood," leading the willing
opposition of many others. It was now the
Court's turn to take the back track. They
yielded to the many and strong objections of
the people, being "forced to desist from that
proceeding."

It was near the time of the conflict on the
oath question that Endicott, at Salem, cut the
cross from the national flag. This unwise act
was prompted, no doubt, by a feeling common
to the Puritans, that this symbol was one of the

relics of Popery. The Court punished Endicott for this act by declaring that he should be incapable of holding any public office for one year. Williams' name has been connected with this act. He undoubtedly preached against Popish symbols, but there is no proof that he advised Endicott's application of his preaching, and as the Court did not blame him in the matter, we may safely assume that he was not to be blamed.

At the Court before which Endicott was cited, a petition was received from the people of Salem concerning some lands in Marblehead which they claimed as theirs. The Court replied, in effect : " You ordained Williams contrary to our wishes, and we wont give you your lands !" The Salem people keenly felt this wrong, and appealed, by letters sent to all the Churches, to the constituents of the members of the Court. It will be remembered that no man could vote who was not a church-member, so the Salem people justly held their brethren in the Churches responsible for what their representatives had done. These letters the Court resented by denying at their next session the representatives from Salem their seats. At a little later time Endicott justified before the

Court these letters, and protested against the unwarranted course of its members. The Court gave the customary reply of arbitrary power, by putting him in prison until he acknowledged his fault in the matter.

CHAPTER VII.

MORE PERILS.

THE Court could not be thus troubled by the Salem people and not consider that their Pastor was in part the troubler. Their worships, at the session which rejected the representatives, summoned Williams before them, " to answer for divers dangerous opinions." They brought up against him the opinions for which he had before been called to answer. In addition, they charged him with believing " that a man ought not to pray with an unregenerate person, though wife or child ; and that a man ought not to give thanks after the sacrament nor after meat."

Unworthy matters to be persistently emphasized, we should say, if Williams really did so ; but no concern of the magistrates any way. Whether he really held the opinions as above stated is not quite certain. It must be remembered that we have only his opponents' rendering of his sentiments. We may not charge them with intentional misrepresentation, but it is plain that the controversy between Williams and them had become too heated for fairness. The time for argument on the part of the authorities had closed, and they informed the Salem people and their minister that at their next session they should expect an acknowledgment of their errors of doctrine and fault of conduct in the matter of the letters and the settling of their Pastor. Failing to do this, sentence against them would be executed.

Williams' health failed under the pressure of his professional duties and these legal vexations. From his sick room he wrote to his Church in seeming heat—perhaps more in sorrow than in anger. He declared to them that, as things stood, "he could not communicate with the Churches in the Bay." He went even further, saying to his brethren and sisters : "If you communicate with them, I will not with you."

"Oppression makes a wise man mad." It may be that Williams was somewhat beside himself in taking the latter position. We doubt not it loosened in a degree the strong cords of affection which had to this moment bound his people to him, and prepared them for the abject submission to the magistrates at his expense, which soon followed.

The Court which was in session in October carried matters with a high hand. Endicott had been disqualified for office for indorsing the letters to the Churches. They now demand the names of all those of Salem who are known to approve of them. Williams was, of course, cited before them, for what was a Court at such a time without his presence? The only charges against him now are the two letters. He boldly defended their contents against the arguments of Hooker, who was appointed to dispute with him. At the close of the discussion the parties remained in the same relation to each other as at its beginning, except a probably wider alienation of feeling.

Failing to secure Williams' submission, the authorities sentenced him to banishment beyond the bounds of their colony. The sentence was to take effect within six weeks. The ministers, as usual, were present by invitation, and all but one voted for banishment.

Mr. Williams returned to Salem with this sentence hanging over him. He found his Church at the feet of the magistrates. We

cannot say how large an influence in bringing
them into this humble position the question of
their litigated lands had, but it is a matter of
record that what was refused because they did
not submit was granted soon after they had
written "an humble submission to the magistrates, acknowledging their fault in joining with
Mr. Williams in that letter to the Churches
against them, etc."

Why should not the Church at Salem have
submitted? The Court, which was only the
other Churches acting through their chosen
representatives, did but require of them the
application of the doctrine which they had imposed upon the Browns, whom they had sent
over the sea for not agreeing in opinion with
them. Very likely they learned by their contest with the Churches that enforced conformity
made occasion for blows which were pleasanter
to give than to receive.

Mr. Williams, forsaken by his Church, and
chidéd by his wife for not yielding, still stood
firm. The people, if they did not agree with
his opinions, admired his character, for an old
historian says: "The whole town of Salem was
in an uproar at the decree of banishment, for

he was esteemed an honest, disinterested man, and of popular talents in the pulpit." Many prepared to show the sincerity of their attachment by following in his wanderings.

The Court so far relented as to extend the time of his departure to the following spring, on conditions that he should not disseminate his opinions. Abstinence from talking of what he believed was never a grace with Williams. He continued to freely ventilate his notions to those who came to his house, and many were made of the same mind, for " they were much taken with the apprehension of his godliness." This would not do. He was cited to Boston " to be shipped." He declined going, saying that it would be at the hazard of his life. The authorities sent a boat round to Salem to carry him on board a ship lying at Nantasket, just ready to sail for England. Williams understood what was intended. The bitterness of the weather made him fear such a voyage. Besides, he had no occasion for a return to the fatherland, believing that God had work for him in America. So when the boat arrived, the prey had escaped.

It is pleasant to record the fact that this

secret escape was prompted by a private, friendly letter from the then ex-Governor Winthrop. The Governor, while acting officially at times against Williams, was, and ever remained, a warm personal friend. In fact, there is no evidence of malice on the part of the Court in these oppressive proceedings, their errors being rather of the head than the heart. The respect, and even love, manifested by many of Williams' prosecutors is not only creditable to them, but shows the intrinsic greatness and excellence of his own character.

CHAPTER VIII.

CAST OUT.

IN going forth into the stormy winter of January, 1636, Mr. Williams left lands of his own, and a house which he had either purchased or built. He left, too, wife and children, the eldest child being but a little over two years of age, and the youngest scarcely three months. The last, born, of course, in the midst of his bitterest conflicts, he named Freeborn. It was a Puritan practice to note some passing event or present feeling by the names given to newborn children. The little Freeborn's name indicated her father's faith that men should be free from their birth.

It does not seem probable that any one accompanied Williams, as he left his home by stealth, as a hunted outlaw. He took a pocket compass to guide him through the pathless forest, which is among the preserved mementoes of his journey. He would, we think, take the Boston road, over which he had so often travcled to answer the citations of the Court, until he reached Saugus, eight or nine miles from his brethren at the Bay, whom he would avoid. Then striking off west for a while, into the unknown and unbroken woods, he finally directed his course due south. He says : " I was sorely tossed for one fourteen weeks in a bitter winter season, not knowing what bread or bed did mean."

What a journey was that ! How often must he have turned back to avoid some impenetrable thicket, or to go round a treacherous swamp, or to find a practicable passage of a running stream ! How sorely he must have been pressed with hunger in the absence of all fruit, and without the possibility of the poor resort to roots ! If he had the means of bringing down the game with the heavy flint-lock gun of those days, (then just displacing the match-lock,) that of itself imposed a heavy burden. No doubt the Indians gave him friendly shelter, but how uncertain as well as unpleasant must have been his nightly resting places ! No wonder that he exclaimed in old age : " I bear to this day in my body the effect of that winter's exposures."

This midwinter's thrusting out of Roger

Williams has been well rendered in poetry by an enthusiastic poet* of Rhode Island, in connection with the whole fancied story of his banishment. He thus sings:

> " So forth he went—even like the dove
> Which earliest left the angel-guarded ark ;
> On weary pinions hovered she above
> The vast of waters heaving wild and dark,
> Over waste realms of death, whilst still she strove
> Some peak emergent from the flood to mark,
> Where she might rest above the billows' sweep,
> And build a stormy home 'mid that unquiet deep."

Through storms, indeed, to build "a stormy home" was Williams journeying. But

> " Still truly does his course the magnet keep—
> No toils fatigue him, and no fears appal ;
> Oft turns he at the glimpse of swampy deep,
> Or thicket dense, or crag abrupt and tall,
> Or backward treads to shun the headlong steep,
> Or pass above the tumbling waterfall. . . .
> Across his path with antlers branching wide,
> The bounding deer oft from the thicket broke ;
> The timid partridge at his rapid stride
> On thundering wings the sheltering bush forsook,
> And the wild turkey foot and pinion plied,
> Or from her lofty boughs uncouthly cried. . . .
> And then night's thickening shades began to fill
> His soul with doubt—for shelter he had none—
> And all the outstretched waste was clad with one

---

* " Whatcheer ; or, Roger Williams in Banishment. By Job Durfee, LL.D."

Vast mantle hoar.   And he began to hear,
At times, the fox's bark, and the fierce howl
Of wolf, sometimes afar—sometimes so near
That in the very glen they seemed to prowl
Where now he, wearied, paused—and then his ear
Started to note some shaggy monster's growl,
That from his snow-clad, rocky den did peer,
Shrunk with gaunt famine in that tempest drear,
And scenting human blood--yea, and so nigh
Thrice did our northern tiger seem to come,
He thought he heard the fagots crackling by,
And saw, through driven snow and twilight gloom,
Peer from the thickets his fierce burning eye,
Scanning his destined prey, and through the broom
Thrice stealing, on his ears the whining cry
Swelled by degrees above the tempest high."

The six weeks of exposure in the wilderness
ended about the first of March. He had reached
the wigwam of his old friend Massasoit. While
residing at Plymouth, Williams, it will be recollected, had often been the guest of this Chief.
Williams had kept the acquaintance fresh and
cordial during the intervening years by friendly
messages, and to the Indian Chief, more welcome presents. He could not, of course, have
foreseen the value to himself of such a friendship. He had, undoubtedly, sought by it only
the religious welfare of the savages. Now it
was in the power of Massasoit to grant him not
only a home, but to aid him in securing a posi-

tion of the widest influence for good. While resting at the royal head-quarters at Mount Hope, near the present town of Bristol, R. I., Williams obtained from him a grant of land now included in the town of Seekonk, in Massachusetts, on the east bank of Seekonk river. True to his principles with regard to the Indian ownership of the land, he regarded the Sachem's deed as sufficient. This certainly was true in equity, unless the old Chief had before bargained it away to the Plymouth colony, who, in fact, now claimed that bank of the river as within their limits.

He began at once to build a house—a cabin, no doubt, somewhat after the fashion of those of American pioneers. He cleared the ground, or sought cleared places, and planted Indian corn. The poet expresses this well:

"Long did this task Sire Williams' cares engage,
 'Twas labor strange to hands like his, I ween,
That had far oftener turned the sacred page,
 Than hewed the trunk or delved the grassy green;
But toils like these gave honor to the sage;
 The ax and spade in no one's hands are mean,
 And least of all in thine—Illustrious Pioneer!"

Some friends had joined him, though his wife and children remained at Salem. The planting

time was now over; the crops were green under
the sun and showers of June. We can safely
imagine that the "Illustrious Pioneer" was
beginning to feel that a quiet home had been
found at last, where, to use his favorite expression, "soul freedom" could be enjoyed, and
where, re-united to his wife and children, he
might worship God under his own vines.

Such was his situation when he says: "I received a letter from my ancient friend Mr.
Winslow, the Governor of Plymouth, professing
his own and others' love and respect to me, yet
lovingly advising me, since I was fallen into the
edge of their bounds, and they were loath to
displease the Bay, to remove to the other side
of the water, and there, he said, I had the country free before me, and might be as free as
themselves, and we should be loving neighbors
together."

This was hard, but kindly intended advice.
There can be no doubt that Winslow and his
associates in the Pilgrim colony sincerely felt
all "the love and respect" for Williams which
they professed. He seems to have at once
acquiesced in the wisdom of the advice, and we
only wonder that he had not thought, before

Landing of Roger Williams.

building and planting within the Plymouth
colony, of the probable displeasure of the Bay.
He must certainly have known, from a two
years' residence in Plymouth, the extent of their
claim. It may be he was not willing to believe,
without this prompting, that the jealous watch-
fulness of Massachusetts over his supposed
heresies could extend to this far-away forest
home.

Without bitterness or complaint, Williams
prepared immediately to abandon the cabin
which his toil had erected, and the fields which
his industry had sown and cultivated, and to
seek another resting place. With five others
he embarked in his canoe, and dropped down
the river, narrowly watching the western bank
for an inviting landing. On approaching a little
cove near Tockwotten, now India Point, friendly
voices saluted them, though they came from a
group of natives. "What cheer, netop!" they
exclaimed, which was a salutation they had
learned from the English, meaning, "How do
you do, friend!" They landed, but were more
pleased with the welcome than the place. Returning to the canoe, they rounded India Point
and Fox Point, and sailed up a beautiful sheet

of water, skirted then by a dense forest, to a spot near the mouth of the Mosasuck river. A spring of pure water which still marks the place was no doubt one of its attractions. Here he commenced again to build, and to prepare for future planting. He gave to the place the name of Providence, as he says : " In grateful remembrance of God's merciful providence to me in my distress." He is well made to say :

"Accept, O Lord, our thanks for mercies past ;
  Thou wast our cloud by day, and fire by night,
Whilst yet we journeyed through the dreary vast ;
  Thou Canaan more than givest to our sight.
Lord ! 'tis possessed, not seen from Pisgah's height.
  We deeply feel this high beneficence ;
And ages far shall o'er our graves recite
  Of thy protecting grace their father's sense,
And, when they name their home, proclaim *Thy Providence !*"

CHAPTER IX.

A STATE PLANTED.

WHEN Williams and his companions were about to make a home at Providence, he was careful to obtain permission from his Indian friends, Canonicus and Miantonomo. These Chiefs, the associated head of the Narragansetts, gave him also a tract of land extending from what is now the head of Providence Bay, south, along its western shore, to Pawtuxet river. It included what is now several towns. He was to use the banks of the rivers to their sources, and the meadows along their basins included within these limits, as pasture land for his cattle. It was but a verbal agreement at first, but so strong was Williams' hold upon their confidence and affection that these savage Chiefs never faltered in their engagement. Two years afterward Williams put their promise into the form of a deed, which they signed with their marks. They say that they deed this land, " In consideration of the many kindnesses and services he hath continually done for us, both with our friends of Massachusetts, as also at Connecticut, and Apaum or Plymouth." These Indian presents to Mr. Williams were after the historic manner of Indian presents : " You give me, and I give you." He found them very burdensome and costly. He let them have his "shallop and pinnance " whenever they desired ; transporting fifty of them at a time. He sometimes lodged fifty under his roof. When he established a trading house near the old Chief's head-quarters he allowed him to help himself to the goods— a permission more generous than wise, we should think. Of course, his Indian Majesty availed himself of the privilege, and voted his white brother a good fellow. When Canonicus lay on his dying bed he sent for Mr. Williams, and declared that it was his dying request to be buried " in Mr. Williams' cloth of free gift." This meant, we suppose, that he wished that his grave apparel should be a suit of English clothes.

Though this was a costly way to Williams in his poverty to get a foot-hold for the Whites in the Narragansett country, it was probably the only one. The old Chief was very jealous of the English, and Williams says : " It was not thousands nor tens of thousands of money could have bought of him an English entrance into this Bay."

Besides the influence of these presents, Williams mentions other advantages which he had as a negotiator with the Indians, among which were these : " A constant, zealous desire to dive into the natives' language. God was pleased to give me a painful, patient spirit to lodge with them in their filthy, smoky hole (even while I lived at Plymouth and Salem) to gain their tongue. I was known by all the Wampanoags and Narragansetts to be a public speaker at Plymouth and Salem, and therefore with them held as a Sachem ; I could debate with them in a great measure in their own language. Lastly, I had the favor and countenance of that noble soul, Mr. Winthrop, whom all Indians respected."

Mr. Williams' first purpose was to go alone into this Indian country. He says : " My sole desire was to do the natives good, and to that end to learn their language, and therefore desired not to be troubled with English company." But seeing " divers of his distressed countrymen, distressed for conscience," " out of pity " he gave leave to several to accompany him.

The demands of the Indians for presents, and the necessities of his removals, had caused Mr. Williams to sell his house and lands at Salem. He built him a cabin, and in the midsummer after his coming to Providence seems to have had his wife and two children with him. But his poverty was great. He had lost the avails of his spring planting by his compelled removal from Seekonk, and want was knocking at his door. This afforded occasion for a pleasing incident, in which we see how good men rise above the alienating differences of opinions. Williams says : " It pleased the Father of spirits to touch many hearts dear to him with many relentings ; among which that great and pious soul, Mr. Winslow, melted, and kindly visited me at Providence, and put a piece of gold into the hands of my wife for our supply."

In such circumstances, a just business resort would have been the sale of the lands he had obtained, at a fair price, to the new-comers, to whom his settlement was a place of refuge. He justly says that these lands " were mine own as truly as any man's coat upon his back." But he gave them away with a lavish hand, not reserving to himself a foot of land "or an inch of voice" more than to his servants or strangers. No wonder that he had years afterward occasion to say, "I have been blamed for thus parting with my lands." It subjected himself and family to many annoyances.

He began this liberal disposing of his grand landed estate only about eight months after it came into his hands. The memorandum, or informal deed, by which it was effected, runs to twelve persons, "loving friends and neighbors," who are named. It conveyed to them equal rights and powers for the trifling sum of thirty pounds sterling! The "major part" of this company thus formed were to have power to admit others "into the same fellowship of vote." Mr. Williams' prodigal liberality further appears in the fact that the thirty pounds named in this deed was not paid—not a penny of it—by these twelve persons admitted to joint ownership and authority. Thirty shillings was demanded of persons afterward admitted, to form a common stock. Out of this Williams received his thirty pounds—a small part indeed of the cost of his gifts to the Indians.

There was, however, by an arrangement appended to the above, some offset to this hard bargain, yet still leaving the original settler but a shadow of compensation. There was some qualified reservation of lands on the southern boundary of the claim, by which he received about eighteen pounds more.

So far, then, as the twelve friends and neighbors were concerned, whom Williams admitted "out of pity," they suffering for the rights of conscience, the lands were "a loving gratuity." Thus it was, as he says, "not unknown to many witnesses in Plymouth, Salem, and Providence, that my time hath not been spent (though as much as any others whatsoever) altogether in spiritual labors and public exercises of the word; but day and night, at home and abroad, on the land and water, at the hoe, at the oar, *for bread.*"

The community thus started would need soon some form of government. Roger Williams drew up the following document as the keel of their ship of State: "We, whose names are here under-written, being desirous to inhabit the town of Providence, do promise to submit ourselves in active or passive obedience to all

such orders or agreements as shall be made for
the public good of the body in an orderly way,
by the major consent of the present inhabitants,
masters of families, incorporated together into
a township, and such others as they shall admit
unto the same, *only in civil things.*"

The last clause, proclaiming liberty of conscience to all, evidenced what was to be the
controlling spirit of the new body politic. It
was inscribed on the keel, as it was to be upon
the flag, of their noble ship.

For a time, until the number had so increased
as to require a greater division of labor in the
government, "the masters of families" met
monthly to exercise "in town meetings" the
functions of law-makers, judges, and executive
offices. A clerk and treasurer were chosen at
each meeting. Offices were a burden, we suppose, and so they took turns in filling them,
instead, as their neighbors of the Plymouth
colony did in certain cases, of imposing a fine for
non-acceptance. Two persons were appointed
to serve through short terms to preside in their
meetings, to see that order was preserved in the
community, to settle disputes, and execute
orders.

This pure democracy lasted several years.
We regret that we cannot treat our readers to
the privilege of looking in upon this assembly
of the entire sovereign people, resolved into a
committee of the whole for governmental purposes. The debates were spicy, no doubt!
The responsibilities of the affairs of State thus
generously divided among the mass would not
oppress any individual. Great freedom in the
proposal of measures, and in their discussion,
was no doubt used, and often summary disposition was made of them. But we cannot draw
such pictures from the records, for either the
transactions were meagerly kept where every-
body was clerk in turn, or they were destroyed
in the burning of the town by the Indians in
after years.

The first settlers planted their corn on old
Indian fields, or on such clear lands as they
found most convenient. But as they became
more numerous the question of where to settle
and how much land may be taken seems to
have been brought before the people. They
then laid out what are now North and South
Main streets, on the east side of the river, and
divided the land eastward into six-acre lots, of

equal breadth. There were, in the course of
time, one hundred and two of these lots. Each
proprietor had one of them on which he built
his house. They were called "plantations;"
hence the name "Providence Plantations,"
which so long designated, in part, the colony.

A nice little property one of these lots would
now make in the goodly modern Providence!
We do not know what the rule of selection
was, but probably the first who came was first
served. That of Roger Williams included the
place where he first landed and built his house.

The policy of having homes thus near together was the same as that adopted in Plymouth
and Salem, and was suggested by the necessity
of combined defense against the Indians. But
each proprietor was voted, in town meeting, out
lots of upland and meadows. The meadows
and higher land, for planting, could seldom be
united in one farm. Hay was a great article
in that day when hay-seed was not in use, and
the good mowing was carefully parceled in
equal lots.

While Williams was disposing of his great
estate on the mainland, he, jointly with Governor Winthrop, purchased of Canonicus the

island of Chibachuweset, in the Narragansett Bay ; they called it Prudence. Williams soon after bought two smaller islands adjacent, and called them Patience and Hope.

CHAPTER X.

FRIENDLY GREETINGS TO MASSACHUSETTS.

WE expressed a regret, in the last chapter, that the records of the town meetings had not been preserved in sufficient fullness to enable us to know the doings and spirit of its monthly meetings. There is one item of its early records preserved, which, of itself, is so unimportant that we might have passed it by but for a spicy incident, described elsewhere, which the fact recorded occasioned. The item is this, under date of May 21, 1637 : " It was agreed that Joshua Verin, upon a breach of a covenant for restraining of the liberty of con- science, shall be withheld from the liberty of voting until he shall declare the contrary."

Governor Winthrop thus reports this Verin affair. The Governor gives it as an illustration of the difficulties arising from the nature of the Providence settlement, and the manner in which its people dealt with them : "At Providence also the devil was not idle. For whereas at their

first coming thither Mr. Williams and the rest
did make an order that no man should be molested for his conscience, now men's wives and
children and servants, claiming liberty hereby
to go to all religious meetings, though never so
often, or though private, upon the week days ;
and because one Verin refused to let his wife
go to Mr. Williams' so often as she was called
for, they required to have him censured. But
there stood up one Arnold, a witty man of their
company, and withstood it, telling them that
when he consented to that order he never intended it should extend to a breach of any ordinance of God, such as the subjection of wives
to their husbands, and he gave divers solid reasons against it. Then one Greene replied that
if they should restrain their wives all the
women of the country would cry out against
them. Arnold answered him thus : Did you
pretend to leave the Massachusetts because
you would not offend God to please men, and
would you now break an ordinance and com-
mandment of God to please women ? Some
were of opinion that if Verin would not suffer
his wife to have her liberty, the Church should
dispose her to some other man who would use

her better. Arnold told them that it was not the woman's desire to go so oft from home, but only Mr. Williams and others. In conclusion, when they would have censured Verin, Arnold told them that it was against their own order, for Verin did that he did out of conscience ; and their order was that no man should be censured for his conscience."

This is quite a curious affair as it thus stands. It was written under the date of December 13, 1638, and we are surprised that Winthrop should have forgotten the following item of a letter * written to him by Mr. Williams the preceding May, the very month of the entry of the Verin case on the town records, and no doubt immediately after it. The case, it will be seen, does not, under Williams' pen, appear so funny as Arnold's wit or Mr. Winthrop's gossiping informer made it : " Sir, we have been long afflicted by a young man, boisterous and desperate, Philip Verin's son, of Salem, who, as he has refused to receive the Word with us (for which we did not molest him) this twelve months, so, because he could not draw his wife, a gracious and modest woman, to the same ungodliness

* " Winthrop Papers." Mass. His. Col. 4. Vol. vi, p. 245.

with him, he hath trodden her under foot, tyrannically and brutishly. She and we long bore this, though, with his furious blows, she went in danger of her life. At last, by a vote of the majority of us, he was discarded from our civil freedom. He will have justice, he clamors, at other courts. I wish he might for a foul, slanderous, and brutish carriage, which God hath delivered him up unto. He will haul his wife with ropes to Salem, where she must needs be troubled and troublesome, as differences stand. She is willing to stay and live with him, or elsewhere, where she may not offend. I shall humbly request that this item be accepted, and he noway countenanced, until, if need be, I further trouble you."

This was not quite the last of young Verin's case. He left the town when he came under its censure, but in 1650 he wrote to its officials, claiming the land which they seem to have considered forfeited by his absence. The town promised him his land if he would come and prove his claim.

The personal relations of Roger Williams and the excellent Governor Winthrop were unfalteringly of the most Christian character, notwithstanding their great differences on some matters of both opinion and conduct. In the same letter by Williams in which he speaks of the Verin annoyance, he congratulates Winthrop on his recovery from sickness. This prostration, which brought him " near to death," the Governor speaks of in his journal. Williams' peculiar style appears in it, as well as his excellent Christian spirit :

'Sir, blessed be the Father of spirits, in whose hand our breath and ways are, that once more I may be bold to salute you, and congratulate your return from the brink of the pit of rottenness! 'What is man that thou shouldest visit him and try him ?' (Job vii.) You are put off to this tempestuous sea again ; more storms await you. The good Lord repair our leaks, fresh up the gales of his blessed Spirit, steady our course by the compass of his own truth, rescue us from all our spiritual adversaries, not only men, but fiends of war, and assure us of our harbor at last, even the bosom of the Lord Jesus.

"Sir, you have many an eye, I presume, lifted up to the hills of mercy for you. Mine might seem superfluous, yet privately and publicly you have not been forgotten, and I hope shall not while these eyes have sight."

A pleasing postscript appears to one of Williams' letters to Winthrop soon after the banishment. It says, Mrs. Williams sends to Mrs. Winthrop, with respects, "a handful of chestnuts," and promises "a larger basket" if she is fond of them. So the "handful" was a modest expression for a basketful, which love was ready to enlarge if the fruit was relished. The postscript was a little thing—little, like the balmy breath of spring which tones down the bitter frost of winter. May not the husbands have owed something of their kind temper toward each other, in the midst of much provocation to sourness, to the courtesies of their wives?

Among the business letters of Williams to Winthrop of this period there are frequent requests made to the Governor to use his good offices in securing from certain parties the payment of debts due Williams. One of these * contains a clause touchingly significant of the humiliating straits to which poverty, imposed by his banishment, had driven the creditor. It declares that the debt in question was due

* "Winthrop Papers," page 212.

for his wife's and his own "best apparel," which had been sold to the debtor.

The following letter to the Governor has the true ring. It is under the date of 1638.

"Sir, I hear of the innovations of your government. The Lord of heaven be pleased to give you faithfulness and courage in his fear! I fear not so much iron and steel as the cutting of our throats with golden knives. I mean that under the pleasing bait of executing justice to the eastward, and the enlargement of authority, beyond all question lies hid the hook to catch your invaluable liberties. Better an honorable death than a slave's life."*

The correspondence of this period between Williams and Winthrop, though generally of a business character, sometimes dwelt upon religious topics—topics, to be sure, which bore upon the question of his banishment. Winthrop in the following extracts from a letter, under the date of 1638, puts some questions to Williams. The questions, it will be seen, are squarely put, and the answers candidly given, though not always, it must be confessed, given in the directest manner. The good men gave

* "Winthrop Papers," page 239.

and took some good hits, and continued in love to each other. Williams says:

"Your queries I welcome, my love forbidding me to surmise that a Pharisee, a Sadducee, or an Herodian wrote them; but that your love and pity framed them as a physician to the sick. . . .

"Your first query then is this:

"'What have you gained by your new found practices?' I confess my gains, cast up in man's exchange, are loss of friends, esteem, maintenance; but what was gain in that respect I desire to count loss for the excellency of the knowledge of Christ Jesus, my Lord. To your beloved selves and others of God's people yet asleep, this witness in the Lord's season, at your waking shall be prosperous, and the seed sown shall arise to the greater purity of God's kingdom and ordinances.

"To myself through his grace my tribulation hath brought some consolation, and more evidence of his love.

"Your second query is, 'Is your spirit as even as it was seven years ago?'

"I will not follow the fashion either in condemning or commending myself. You and I

stand at one dreadful, dreadful tribunal ! yet
what is past I desire to forget, and to press forward toward the mark of the prize of the high
calling of God in Christ.

"And for the evenness of my spirit, I hope
I more long to know and do his holy pleasure
only, and to be ready not only to be banished,
but to die in New England for the name of the
Lord Jesus.

"Toward yourselves I have hitherto begged
of the Lord an even spirit, and hope ever shall,
as first, reverently to esteem, and tenderly to
respect the persons of many hundreds of you :
secondly, to rejoice to spend and be spent in
any service (according to my conscience) for
your welfare ; thirdly, to rejoice to find out the
least swerving in judgment or practice from the
help of any, even the least of you ; lastly, to
mourn daily, heavily, unceasingly, till the Lord
look down from heaven, and bring all his precious stones into one New Jerusalem.

"Your third query is, 'Are you not grieved
that you have grieved so many ?'

"To which I say with Paul, I vehemently
sorrow for the sorrow of any of Zion's daughters, who should ever rejoice in her King ; yet

7

I must (and O that I had not cause!) grieve because so many of Zion's daughters see not and grieve not for their souls' defilements. . . .

"You thereupon propound a fourth, 'Do you think the Lord hath utterly forsaken us?'

"I answer, Jehovah will not forsake his people for his great name's sake. (1 Sam. 12.) That is, the fire of his love toward those whom once he loved is eternal, like himself; and thus, far be it from me to question his eternal love to you. . . .

"Sir, you request me to be free with you, and therefore blame me not if I answer your request, desiring the like payment from your own dear hand at any time, in any thing.

"And let me add that among all the people of God, wheresoever scattered about Babel's banks, either in Rome or England, your case is the worst by far, because while others of God's Israel tenderly respect such as desire to fear the Lord, your very judgment and conscience lead you to smite and beat your fellow-servants, and expel them your coasts.

"Sir, your fifth query is: 'From what spirit and to what end do you drive?'

"Concerning my spirit, as I said before, I

could declaim against it.   But whether the
spirit of Christ Jesus, for whose visible kingdom
and ordinances I witness, or the spirit of Antichrist, against whom only I contest, do drive me,
let the Father of spirits be pleased to search ;
and you also, worthy sir, be pleased by the word
to search.   And I hope you will find that, as
you say you do, I also seek Jesus who was nailed
to the cross."

CHAPTER XI.

INDIAN NEIGHBORS.

ROGER WILLIAMS had not turned his
steps toward the Narragansett Bay to
found a State. This he expressly declares.
Grand as this purpose would have been, he
sought an end even greater than this. It was
the conversion of the Indians. We have already seen that to this end he had, under circumstances of great privation, studied their
language. His correspondence with them when
he was at Salem shows that this was the burden of his desire. But for this we think he
would have been willing for his brethren at the
Bay to have shipped him, as they purposed, to
England.

Let us glance, then, at these Indian neighbors who are, henceforth, to be his people.

The *Massachusetts*, who dwelt chiefly about
the bay of that name, seem not to have been
a prominent tribe, though Williams, from his
contact with them at times, must have la-

bored considerably for them. The Pokano-
kets, who were included in the territory of the
Plymouth colony, were more important, including some smaller tribes ; among these were
the *Wampanoags*, the immediate tribe of Massasoit and his famous son, Philip. The *Narragansetts* inhabited nearly all of the present State
of Rhode Island, including the islands of the
bay, Block Island, and the east end of Long
Island. The *Pequots*, with whom the *Mohegans*
became blended, occupied the whole of Connecticut. Our story will have much to do with
these tribes, as we follow Williams in his efforts
to do them good. We shall see him at one
time exerting his great influence for the protection of his own countrymen, and, at others,
turning aside the terrible shafts of war from
the Red Man.

At a time not distant from the coming of the
May Flower, the Narragansetts were the ruling
tribe. They were among the tribes of eastern
New England what Judah was among the tribes
of Israel. They might well have inscribed a
lion upon their banner, for at their roaring all
the swarthy dwellers in the forest trembled.
Tribute came to their treasury from the Merri-

mac river, all along the coast of Massachusetts
and Rhode Island, and even from portions of
Long Island.   How long this sway lasted, and
exactly when it began to decline, we do not
know.   Their tradition runs as follows, which
is quite as likely to be true as much that is
written in grave volumes as history.   In fact,
it may be regarded as the received Narragansett
history.   Tashtapack, the ancestor of the old
sachem who reigned at the time of the coming
of the Pilgrims, "was a mighty man of valor"
—the Alexander of his day.   Like the conquerors of the old world, he overturned the kingdoms about him, and built for himself an em-
pire.   Having done this, he surrounded himself
with great splendor in his palace, called by the
curious looking and sounding name *Sachimua-
commock*.   He had one son and one daughter.
He was, of course, very proud of them, and
scorned to match them in marriage with any of
his subjects.   He looked about him through
the courts of the neighboring countries, very
much as kings do in like cases now, but he
could see no prince or princess worthy, in his
esteem, to marry into his family.   So he did
the foolish and unnatural thing of marrying

his son and daughter to each other. Their
sons were many, one of whom was Canonicus,
who still reigned when Williams came to Providence. He was a wise, peaceable sachem,
though he once did a foolish thing which his
ignorance might well excuse. He tried to
scare the Pilgrims. He sent them a bundle of
arrows tied up with a snake skin, which meant
"We'll fight you." The Pilgrims sent the skin
back full of powder, which said "We are not
afraid." No harm was done, but Canonicus
and his warriors were terribly scared when
they received the powder.

Canonicus, who, at the time of our story,
was an old man, had associated in the government with him his nephew, the mild Miantonomo. This nephew will come before us in stirring and tragic scenes.

Just before the Pilgrims landed, a pestilence
swept away many thousands of the Indians.
Massasoit, who had ruled over ten tribes, and
was independent of all, lost his people by this
disease, and, in consequence, became tributary
to Canonicus. His treaty with the Pilgrims
was made wisely, with an eye to his own
interest, for under their protection he qui-

ctly withdrew from under the Narragansett rule.

The Narragansetts had, on the coming of the Whites, lost their military character, though, as we have seen, still exercising large authority. They had, to a great extent, laid aside the bow and spear for the peaceful pursuits of agriculture and manufacture. They were the Indian Yankees. They set up the first mint known among the natives, from which they sent out money made of shells. They had superior skill in making implements out of stone, in building canoes, in manufacturing beads and ornamental belts, and various forms of earthenware. They had large tracts of land under cultivation, so that town was joined to town through a great distance. Their sachems were, of course, rich in corn, and the old historians speak of their occasional presents of a thousand bushels to a single friend!

Though thus peaceful, they could muster, it is said, for the war path, five thousand men.

The general character of the Indian tribes is well known. They were warm friends, but bitter, implacable enemies. Their minds were very dark, of course, on the subject of religion, and concerning the true God. Like all heathen, they learned the vices of the white men much more readily than their virtues. Gambling was a native vice, but drunkenness they learned from the pale faces, and became, if possible, greater adepts than their teachers in this refined art of misery.

The most wonderful thing connected with the Indians was their language. We might expect this to be scanty and cramped in its ability to express varying shades of thought. But such was not the fact. It was regular, copious, rich in forms, and wonderfully flexible in combination and nice discrimination. It has been favorably compared by scholars to the ancient Greek, in all the qualities which make a first-class language.

The languages and dialects of the continent of America have been estimated at 1,214, more than a third of the entire number of the world.

Yet the native languages of North America have been reduced to four classes only—the Karalit of the extreme north, the Floridian of the southern frontier of the United States, the Delaware of the east, and the Iroquois of the west. Of course, the dialects of each were

many. Those of New England were a variety
of the Delaware language. Roger Williams
gave his special attention to the Narragansett
tongue, in which he became more proficient,
probably, than any white man of his generation. He says that, " With this I have entered
into the secret of those countries wherever
English dwell, about two hundred miles between
the French and Dutch plantations. There is
a mixture of this language north and south of
my abode, about six hundred miles ; yet within
two hundred miles aforesaid their dialects do
exceedingly differ, yet not so but (within that
compass) a man may, with this. help, converse
with thousands of natives all over the country.

An example of the power of inflection of Indian languages is given in a word of forty-one
letters of our alphabet, whose translation into
English requires eighteen words. It is regu-
larly formed according to fixed rules !

After this brief glance at the neighbors of
Roger Williams, we return to follow his varying experience while trying to discharge his
duty both to them and his white brethren.
With distinguished Indian chiefs his history
will make us further acquainted.

CHAPTER XII.

THE WAR CLOUD.

A WAR cloud hung over all the New England colonies when Roger Williams commenced his settlement in Providence. The Pequots of Connecticut, a fierce people full of savage cruelty, had from the first looked with jealousy upon the coming of the Whites. But the Narragansetts, the ancient enemies of the Pequots, held them in check by their more friendly bearing toward the pale faces. In 1634 the captain and all the crew, numbering ten men, of a vessel on the Connecticut river were murdered. The murderers fled to the Pequots, who gave them shelter, though it is not certain they were of that nation. This brought Massachusetts' messengers to their door demanding satisfaction. With evident reluctance the Pequots paid the penalty imposed and made peace, but nursed their wrath and watched their opportunity.

Thus the relations of these savages stood to

the Whites in the summer of 1636, when Williams began his struggle for a new home.   In
July, John Oldham, and two English boys, and
two Narragansett Indians, went on a trading
voyage up the Connecticut.   Oldham was a
daring trader of doubtful character, and in bad
repute with both Indians and Whites.   On their
return they touched at Block Island, where Oldham was murdered.   The murderers fled to the
usual refuge in such cases, the camp of the
Pequots.   This time there were evident signs
of complicity in the crime on the part of the
Narragansetts.

When the news of this murder reached Boston their martial spirit was roused.   Fortu-
nately, messengers from Canonicus almost immediately followed the arrival of the news.
They bore a letter from their trusted friend
Roger Williams to Governor Vane, and were
accompanied by the two Indians who were with
Oldham.   Soon after, the two boys were sent
to their homes, and another letter from Mr.
Williams assured the Governor that Miantonomo had sent men to Connecticut, and recovered
them and the property, and that he would
avenge the death of Oldham.   The faithful

chief sachems thus cleared their skirts of this blood, and showed that if any of their dependent tribes had taken a part in the crime it was without their knowledge.

So the blow from the Bay fell on the Pequots only. John Endicott was sent with ninety men in three small vessels, to Block Island. Landing on the island, he burnt the wigwams, staved the canoes, and then left for the Connecticut river. At Saybrook they received a reinforcement of twenty men, after which they sailed for the Pequot head-quarters at the mouth of the Thames river. Their Chief, Sassacus, was absent. Endicott attacked and burned their town, killing some of its defenders. He then burned the forsaken wigwams on the opposite side of the river, broke up the canoes, and returned home without the loss of a man. Endicott was sharply criticised, many thinking it was an inglorious war thus far on the part of the Whites. Certain it was that the Pequot blood was up. They scattered during the following winter, firebrands and death through the English settlements of Connecticut. They sent embassadors to the Narragansetts, proposing an alliance for the extermination of the white-faced intruders.

The Pequots hated the Narragansetts much, but the English more. It was the most perilous hour the New England colonies had yet seen. Sassacus appeared at the Council fire of the grave and cautious Canonicus. His eloquence was fired by the smart which Endicott had inflicted upon his nation, and by a deep conviction that his people or the Whites must go down. He urged upon the Council the fact that the cause of the Indian tribes was a common cause, and that they must now fight for the soil their fathers had left them, for their own lives and for those of their wives and children, and for the graves of their ancestors.

Such truthful arguments from a burning heart could but render doubtful, at least, the decision of the Narragansetts. At this crisis, Williams appeared among them. No other white man could have gone as safely. He was shielded by the love of the Narragansetts from the arrow and knife of the enraged Pequots. The authorities at Boston, alarmed at the pitchy blackness which the war cloud had assumed, turned for aid to their banished brother. They knew they could confide in him in this their hour of need, and in this they paid him the highest compliment.

Williams' own pen well describes his negotiations and their results : " Upon letters from
the Governor and Council at Boston requesting
me to use my utmost and speediest endeavors,
to break and hinder the league labored for by
the Pequots and Mohegans against the English,
the Lord helped me immediately to put my life
into my hand, and scarce acquainted my wife, to
ship myself alone in a poor canoe, and to cut
through a stormy wind with great seas, every
minute in hazard of life, to the Sachem's house.
Three days and nights my business forced me
to lodge and mix with the bloody Pequot embassadors, whose hands and arms methought
recked with the blood of my countrymen, murdered and massacred by them on Connecticut
river, and from whom I could nightly look for
their bloody knives at my own throat also. God
wondrously preserved me, and helped me to
break to pieces the Pequots' negotiations and
design, and to make and finish by many
travels and changes the English league with
the Narragansetts and Mohegans against the
Pequots."

In consequence of these negotiations by
Williams, Governor Vane, of Massachusetts,

invited Narragansett embassadors to Boston to officially arrange the treaty. In response to this call the junior Chief, Miantonomo, with two sons of Canonicus, one other Sachem, and twenty attendants, went on the 21st of October, 1636, to Boston. They were received with the deference due to "a high contracting party," with military escorts and salutes, and when the treaty was completed they were dismissed with the same honors.

Through a significant incident, Roger Williams came in for further service and honor before the consummation of this important business. Because the Indians could not perfectly understand the terms of the treaty, it was sent to him to interpret it to them. This showed the confidence of all parties in him, and the honest intentions of the Boston officials toward the Indians. The treaty was one of alliance, offensive and defensive, against the Pequots. The Pequots, though thus abandoned even by the Mohegans, and left single-handed in the fight, resolved, with more bravery than discretion, to abide the result of war. The war tempest was upon the colonies.

CHAPTER XIII.

THE WAR TEMPEST.

WHEN, some months after this treaty was completed, the Boston authorities were intending an attack on the Pequots, Williams went immediately to the camp of Canonicus. He informed him what the intentions and preparations of his white allies were. He found the usually placid Chief morose and distant. Some intermeddling "ill-willer" had been whispering frightful stories in his ears. He had been told that the English had been concerting to send the plague among the Indians, and thus in a short and speedy way to get rid of such troublesome neighbors, and save all bloody and expensive wars! "The plot includes even me," growled the poor old man; and the most bitter part of the whole story was that his trusted friend Williams was consenting to the proposed bloody tragedy! No wonder that Williams saw cause for "bestirring" himself. He remained long in the wigwam of Canonicus, pointing out

8

to him the impossibility of the alleged scheme, and convincing him of the great wrong that the story did him and his white brethren. "Through the mercy of God," he says, "I sweetened his spirit, and convicted him that the plague and other sicknesses are in the hands of the one God."

Miantonomo was managed by Williams with even greater ease and success. He kept his barbarous court at one time in his house. He thus secured his confidence and good-will in the interests of the English. Taking the advantage of this confidence, he says he "fished with industry for instructions from them as to how the Whites could best fight the Red Men." It must be recollected that what is known so well now as the Indian method of fighting was unknown to the colonists then. This information, which must have been of great value, Williams dispatched at once to Boston to his friend Winthrop. The suggestions were in substance that they must strike the Pequots suddenly and then feign a retreat, and then, when they were thrown off their guard, rush down upon them ; and this must be done not two or three days and then off, but for three weeks or a month. They said that the Pequots would be on the look-out for the English vessels on their coast, and when one appeared they would all flee—old people, women and children, as well as warriors—to a swamp in the rear of their settlement, two or three miles from the shore. This swamp was a great and marvelous one, called Ohomowauke—that is, owl's nest. This "owl's nest" was a refuge from which the Pequots expected to rush out upon the white foe if they would consent to be surprised. But the Narragansetts counseled the Boston men not to allow Indian "surprise parties" to visit them, they being less agreeable than those of the same name in modern times. But they advised that these surprises be given rather than received, which was generous, and that the time be in the still watches of the night; that the manner be with ambush men to cut off the flight to the swamp, and that the things carried be powder and shot and burning fire-brands! All this advice Canonicus and his chiefs passed along through Williams to Boston, with much more of the same sort. But they modestly suggested, in a postscript to Williams' letter, that commodities of a wholly different sort would best please the Nar-

ragansetts; in fact, "If any things be sent
to the princes," says Williams, "I find that
Canonicus would gladly accept of a box of eight
or ten pounds of sugar; indeed, he told me he
would thank Mr. Governor for a box full."
There, that was sensible. A box full of sugar
in one's lock-up is twice as good as a flaming
torch to one's roof at midnight, accompanied by
the smell of "villainous saltpeter."

The Pequots soon convinced all concerned
that they had not been consulted in the nice
little arrangement which had been made through
Mr. Williams. They commenced the campaign
in Connecticut by cutting off the men in the
fields, and the women and the children in their
homes. They put some to cruel tortures. The
tomahawk was a coming invention, and the
bloody scalping-knife was a weapon whose use
was soon to be learned from the higher civiliza-
tion of the French on the north-eastern frontier. As it was, the Pequots did their murderous war-work quite well for savages. They
gave the fort at the mouth of the Connecticut
a surprise party. They gave straggling white
boat clubs their emphatic salutations. They
made a massacre at Wethersfield a well-remem-

bered event; and the capture of two white girls
at another time, after the murder of their
friends, they made the pathetic theme of many
a fireside story. In fact, the Pequots were
about. Connecticut, whose three little towns,
Hartford, Wethersfield, and Windsor, had been
organized only about a year, mustering in all
considerably less than two hundred men, was
soon in the field with her forces. Massachusetts
prepared to launch, like a thunderbolt, upon
the foe her mighty army of one hundred and
twenty men! Think of the Bay State in her
infancy, ye mighty warriors of the late Rebellion, to whom five thousand soldiers were a
skirmishing party!

General Stoughton, with the Bay forces,
marched toward the front by the way of Providence. Mr. Williams entertained him at his
house, and says: "I used my utmost care that
all his officers and soldiers should be well ac-
commodated among us." He accompanied the
troops to the country of their Narragansett allies, and by his influence established a mutual
confidence between the Red and White warriors.
He then returned to Providence, and acted
through the war as the valued and almost indis-

pensable medium of communication between Massachusetts and her army and the Indians.

Connecticut sent Captain John Mason to the scene of conflict with ninety men, attended by Uncas, chief of the Mohegans, with sixty of his warriors. It is said that the Pequots could muster nearly a thousand fighting men. They had two fortified villages, one on the Mystic river, a small stream running into the eastern part of Long Island Sound. The other, a short distance from it, was the head-quarters of Sassacus, the Pequot leader-in-chief.

Captain Mason marched to Saybrook, at the mouth of the Connecticut, where the Mohegans performed some valiant deeds in killing a few of the enemy, thus demonstrating their fidelity to the Whites, and proving, to themselves at least, their amazing prowess.

At Saybrook, Mason, being re-inforced by Captain Underhill, who had been sent from Massachusetts with twenty men, took the most of his troops and sailed for Narragansett Bay, intending to surprise the Pequots by a land at-tack in their rear. They reached a harbor on Saturday, and spent the Sabbath on shipboard in religious exercises. Their Chaplain, the Rev.

Mr. Stone, who was both devout and brave, led their devotions. The two following days they rode out at anchor a terrific storm, which was a poor preparation for a two days' weary march across an unbroken country. They were accompanied by a frightened force of the warriors of Canonicus, sixty trembling Mohegans, and a straggling band of Niantics. On Thursday night they encamped near Fort Mystic. The weary Englishmen slept soundly. When, long before day, Mason awakened them, they paused, before rushing to the deadly conflict, for a season of prayer under the lead of the chaplain.

The Pequot fort was a circular area of an acre or two, inclosed by trunks of trees, twelve feet high, set in the ground. They were too near together to admit entrance, and wide enough apart for the arrow shots of the Indian defenders. Within were seventy wigwams. The four hundred occupants of the fort spent that fatal night in carousals. They had seen from the headlands the vessels of Mason and Underhill sail away eastward. No doubt they indulged in merry jeers at the expense of the "woman-hearted" English, whom they fondly dreamed were scudding away home. The two

entrances, on opposite sides, were well fortified. Through these Mason and Underhill,
each with half the English forces, were to push
forward to the center area. Most of the Indian
allies had taken counsel of their fears, and
melted away. The remaining faithful ones
were stationed around the fort to cut off any
attempting to escape.

The calm bright moon, whose silver rays
have been shed upon so many bloody scenes,
lighted the approach to the sallyport. When
Mason was within a few feet a dog barked, and
aroused the unfaithful sentinels. The shout of
"*Owanux! Owanux!*" ran through the camp,
—"Englishmen! Englishmen!" No surprised
village of White men could be thrown into
greater consternation at the terrific Indian war-
whoop than were the Mystic fort revelers at
this moment. Mason, with sixteen men, sprang
forward at the instant, and forced the entrance.
Underhill had been equally successful on the
opposite side. The inmates, like emmets on a
burning log, ran in terror in every direction.
But whichever way they turned was death.
Broadsword and musket were too slow in their
work of destruction. Mason gave the thrilling

order, " Fire the wigwams." Flaming brands were hurled at the matting and thatched roofs. A north-east wind was blowing, and the flames spread like our prairie fires. Women and children, alike with the strong warriors, perished on that terrible night. Some, climbing the parapets, were shot down. Others, failing to break through the English lines, turned with frenzied desperation and threw themselves into the not less merciful flames. A few rushed upon the invaders, and died with heroic bravery. Those, with few exceptions, who considered themselves fortunate in escaping beyond the burning fort, were shot down by the co-operating Indians, who were brave now in the presence of a defeated and terror-stricken foe.

The number of Indians who perished is variously stated at from four to seven hundred. "Not above five escaped out of our hands," says Captain Underhill.

Captain Mason had a narrow escape. An Indian quite near him leveled his arrow and drew the string with a strong hand, to send it through him. The captain's orderly sprang to the side of the savage, and cut the bow-string.

The English lost only two killed, but a quarter of their force was wounded.

The action lasted but about an hour. A nation, once proud and defiant, and ruling over many others, perished in that hour, for the star of the Pequots had set forever. How terrible is war! How desolating are its visitations, and how unlike those of the Prince of Peace!

CHAPTER XIV.

AFTER THE STORM.

THE scenes after the sweep of a tornado, if not so terrific as at the moment of its activity, are often more appalling. Prostrate trees, demolished houses, mangled corpses, and homeless and agonized men and women, are some of the features of the darkly-shaded picture presented.

It was thus after the war tempest. Mason had lost by death only two men, but half of his number were bleeding and helpless. He marched from the smoldering ruins of the Pequot fort toward the mouth of the Pequot river, (now the Thames,) where he had arranged to meet his vessels. The weather was excessively hot, and the exhausted men, burdened with their wounded companions, dragged through the impeded forest pathway with slow footsteps. Their provisions were nearly exhausted, so that hunger was added to weariness. There had been a great scarcity of all sorts of provisions among their families at home. So the soldiers sadly mourned not only a scarcity of bread, but of rum! They say, "We had but one pint of strong liquors among us in our whole march!" We are persuaded it was a pint too much. But they did not think so, for, having drank that up, we presume in carefully divided portions, they passed the bottle round to be smelled of! They declare, "The very smelling to the bottle would presently recover such as fainted away."

Nor was this want of bread all ; their ammunition was nearly expended, and the other fortified place of the Pequots lay only a little west of their line of march. As the Whites plodded along under these disheartening circumstances, they saw approaching them three hundred Pequots from this fort. They had heard of the fate of their countrymen in the assault of the night, and they were raving with revenge. Mason, who seemed never at loss in emergencies, hired his Indian allies to carry his wounded, inspirited his companions, and presented a bold front. The Pequots, fearing the Whites, turned upon a detachment of fifty of his Narragansett helpers. True to his friends, Mason generously detached Underhill, who succeeded in rescuing them and bringing them back. At length Mason reached an eminence which over-looked the harbor, and his eyes were gladdened by a sight of his vessels just coming to anchor. The friends on the land and sea gave immediate signals of recognition. Thanks were at once rendered to God for his preserving care. That night the exhausted conquerors rested safely on board their vessels. They found there Captain Patrick, from Massachusetts, with forty fresh men. They had arrived in the Narragansett Bay too late to join Mason, and so came round in his vessels.

Underhill took the wounded and sailed for the Connecticut river, while Mason undertook to complete his work of destruction on the land. He sent detachments to protect the towns, and, with the rest of his little army, scoured the country, and arrived at the fort at Saybrook toward the last of the week. He was received by its commander with " many big guns," and the warriors kept their Sabbath with psalms, thanksgiving, and prayer.

The remnant of the doomed Pequots col-lected in their remaining fort, of which we have

spoken. A month's lull in the tempest which
was sweeping them away gave them time to
rally their fainting spirits. They entertained,
in stormy debate, the question whether to fall
upon the English or upon the Narragansetts, or
to seek in flight a hiding-place farther west.
Burning their wigwams and supplies, and gathering together their little ones and old people,
they prepared to turn their backs on the homes
of their childhood, their hunting and fishing
grounds, and the graves of their fathers, and
seek a home toward the setting sun. They had
proceeded but a short distance, reaching a spot
a little west of where New Haven now stands,
when Captain Stoughton arrived at the mouth
of the Pequot river, and landed one hundred
and twenty Massachusetts men. Here he
joined Mason, who had forty men, and the combined force started in pursuit. They found the
Pequots in a spot which was surrounded by
quagmires, rendering approach to it difficult
and dangerous. The English paused, sent a
flag of truce, and asked for the surrender of the
old men, women, and children, as they were
"loath to destroy them." This was granted,
and was merciful on the part of the assailants

and wise on the part of the Indians. The morning which followed was foggy. Taking advantage of this, the warriors made a sudden attack on Mason's line, and seventy of them broke through and escaped. After this brief struggle Mason's conquest was easy, though for the first time in the English encounters with the Indians they had to face a few muskets. One hundred and eighty prisoners were taken, besides those surrendered in the parley.

The war was virtually closed. Indeed, the Mystic fort fight had decided the issue. Sassacus, the Pequot Chief, no mean foe, seeing his nation ruined, fled, with a few of his men, to the brutal Mohawks on the Hudson river, by whom he was murdered. The scattered remnants of his people were hunted from their hiding-places as pioneer settlers hunt beasts of prey. The other Indian tribes seemed to owe them a grudge, and every-where devoured them, as wolves are said to devour the disabled members of their pack. They continued for some time to bring Pequot heads or hands as trophies to Boston. Eight hundred had been slain in the war, and some delivered themselves up at Hartford on condition that their lives should be spared. The miserable remnant of the extinguished nation were divided out as slaves among their conquerors, both Indian and English.

Thus was annihilated the first of the long line of Indian tribes which have passed away before the more powerful white man, leaving the solemn question of responsibility of what was done for the discussion of after generations, and for settlement at God's righteous bar. The savage was animated by the thought that he was fighting for the territory inherited from his fathers or acquired by his bravery. The English were inspired by a dread of the midnight murderer among their wives and children. The result of the contest brought a forty-years' peace to all the colonies.

. After the swamp fight Stoughton returned to Massachusetts, having lost one man only. A day of thanksgiving was observed throughout New England. In Boston a sermon was preached, after which the returned heroes of war were feasted. The little army of Connecticut, dispersed over the plantations, hung their muskets, with their inseparable powder-horns, in some conspicuous place in the large kitchen, and on winter evenings repeated to willing ears the story of the Pequot war.

We have seen the part which Roger Williams took in this conflict. He was one of the acknowledged saviors of the colonists. His wisdom foresaw the evil, and aided his brethren in hiding themselves. His services at home were as positively useful, if not as greatly so, as any military leader's in the field. His friend Winthrop, in Boston, saw this, and generously stepped forward with the proposal of his recall from banishment as an acknowledgment for his services. Other influential men sympathized with him. But the stern consistency of the rulers prevailed. They had not banished him out of dislike to his person, but out of hatred and fear of his doctrines. They might love his person more now, but they did not hate his opinions less. Nor had Williams abated any of his convictions or persistency in the direction of "soul liberty." So it was well for them to live apart, however wrong was the cause of that separation.

It happened with our fathers as it has with their children, that war left its dreadful scars. The smoke of the battle had scarcely blown away before a serious jealousy sprung up be-

tween the Boston authorities and their Indian
allies. The reader will not be surprised that
the principal cause was the Pequot slaves which
had been divided among the victors. Yotaash,
a brother of Miantonomo, was sent to Boston to
represent the Narragansetts' view of the contention. He returned with a letter to the Chiefs
containing complaints and threatenings. As in
all such cases, Williams came in as the trusted
peace-maker. He accompanied Yotaash to the
Narragansett head-quarters. The council fire
was lighted, and the "big talk" commenced.
Williams interpreted the governor's letter, faith-
fully rendering grievances and threats, between
the several clauses of which no doubt the Indians put in many an "umph!" Williams, when
the reading had closed, held up to them the
treaty, and took at the same time a straw, and
broke it in two or three pieces, signifying to
them that they had thus broken it. Canonicus
answered that Mr. Governor would see they
were honest and faithful when he understood
their answer. And still further, he insisted,
though he didn't like to contend with his
friends, that the English had broken the treaty
on their part since the war.

Then followed the statements of the particular cases of grievance on each side, and the replies, Williams urging the English view. The statements are greatly confused in Mr. Williams' letter, but it seemed to be in substance this: Some Indian women belonging to the Massachusetts people had escaped to the Narragansett country. It was a genuine case—perhaps the first on the continent—of runaway slaves. Canonicus said he had never seen any, but hearing of some "in his parts, bade carry them back to Mr. Governor." Miantonomo said that he had heard of six only, four of whom were brought before him, at which he was angry, and ordered "a rendition" (as we should say) through Mr. Williams, to whom he bid his servants carry them. The servants seemed reluctant to do the dirty business, and, after having searched for the other two runaways, returned answer that the women were lame and could not travel. This statement Williams acknowledges had been sent to him, as averred in the Council, accompanied with a request to send men to bring away the fugitives. Williams seems to have thought that this was a dodge, as most likely it was, since we know that runaway slave cases did in later years breed dodges. So Williams returned answer that he had no men to send, and that the Indian sheriffs must do the business. It would seem that at the time of the sitting of this Council the said runaways had not been returned, which no doubt was both a grievance to the Whites, and a cause of one of the "threats." When pressed to know why this had not been done, Miantonomo called Williams' attention to a fact which he well knew, that the time since the demand had been passed by the Indians " in strange solemnities, in which the Chiefs ate nothing by day and the whole country feasted by night," in honor of the late victories. " But now," says the plausible Sachem, "I will have the country searched for them. I do not want the squaw runaways."

Williams promptly replied that he had sent over to beg one. But the wide-awake Sachem was not floored. Either the facts in the case were favorable, or his inventive wit was equal to the occasion. He replied that the Pequot slave whom he desired was a daughter of a deceased friend who had once shown him a great favor, and that he wished to obtain and liberate the daughter for the father's sake.

Williams next, in behalf of his Boston friends, charged the Narragansetts with forsaking the English in the war, and leaving them without a guide. Miantonomo replied that many hundreds of them had stuck to the English in life and death, by which Uncas and the Mohegans were kept from turning against them as he knew they wanted to do and might now. He further cited a case in which two of his men were faithful guides.

Having thus repelled the accusations of his white friends, Miantonomo turns upon them with the following case: His brother, Yotaash, had triumphed over the Pequots in a big skirmish and taken twenty men, among whom was a great Sachem, accompanied by sixty squaws. They had killed three men in the fight. The prisoners they bound, watching them all night, and delivering them to the English in the morning. While they yet remained in the custody of the Whites, Miantonomo came up with his forces, and was very proud, of course, of his brother's success. He at once hastened to the house to see the big captive Chief. " But," he exclaimed, " ciuse wetompatimucks! did ever friend deal so with friend?" He was thrust at with a

pike, and pushed rudely away. "What," exclaimed the indignant Chief, "if we had dealt
so with Mr. Governor?" Mr. Williams urged
that he must have been unknown to the guards.
But the injured chieftain would not admit the
apology, declaring that the insult was so great
that his men desired to be gone.

Williams, in closing his narrative of the
Council, says to Mr. Winthrop, "I dare not
stir coals!" He affirms that he knew that some
Whites had greatly injured the Indians, who in
their ignorance attributed the wrong to all the
English. He speaks a word of caution to both
Massachusetts and Connecticut, and promises
further mediation.

One can but see the kind hand of Providence
in placing Williams between the colonists and
the Indians. Many lives must thereby have
been saved. In view of the irritation of both
parties, he exclaims, "Blessed be the Lord that
things are no worse!"

CHAPTER XV.

A BREEZE FROM ANOTHER QUARTER.

AT the close of the war with the Pequots Roger Williams found his position at Providence one of increasing responsibility and interest. This was so not only in regard to the relation of the colonists to the Indians, but in reference to the relation of the colonists to each other. He had purposed, as we have seen, to shut himself up in the wilderness to win to Christ the Red Men. The providence of God was setting his light on a hill to be seen of all men. New settlements began to be formed about him, and his own rapidly expanded. He was unavoidably drawn into social, religious, political, and commercial relations to the new-comers, and we must follow his history a while in this connection.

We shall not understand the conduct and position of Williams unless we know somewhat, at least, about the character of the new set-tlers, and the immediate occasion of their coming into his region. Let us, then, glance at these topics.

While Massachusetts was threatened with Indian combinations against her, and during the entire conflict with the Pequots, she was fighting a foe more to be dreaded. This foe was internal dissension. Her social and political institutions, not yet consolidated by time nor knit together by the growing wisdom of long experience, were shaken by it to their foundations. The story is a long and complicated one. It has been told often, and always, of course, with some shadings by the writers' own point of observation. We shall state it only so far as is necessary to the clear understanding of our narrative, without expecting to do it any better or more candidly than others have done.

About the time that Williams returned to Salem from Plymouth large numbers of emigrants landed at Boston. They brought news of plots against the liberties of the colony. King Charles was ruling without a Parliament. But this was not all, nor the worst fact concerning his government. Bishop Laud, of whom a distinguished English critic has said that "He was the most worthy of the contempt of the nation of any person in British history," was made virtual primate. He neither carefully studied equity in the ends he sought, nor decency in the means of reaching them. These new emigrants brought well-attested grounds of belief that Bishop Laud and his friends intended to annihilate the colony charter—in fact, that of the Plymouth people too—parcel out the lands among themselves, and establish themselves in the New World, monarchs of all they surveyed. They would, of course, seek some pretense for doing this, and flourish it before the world in pious phraseology. And it was not difficult, of course, to find pretenses, for the wolves which quarrel with the lambs are never at a loss for reasons.

Such was the evil news from abroad. But some writers think, and most of the Boston rulers were led to think, that one of these emigrant vessels of the fall of 1634 brought something worse than the news of the plottings of the Archbishop. It brought Mrs. Ann Hutchinson. She seems to have been a woman of strong will, much culture, great fluency of speech, abundant confidence, and keen logical powers. She added to these very emphatic professions of interest in the care of her own, and of others' spiritual interest. We may not say that it was not a sincere and genuine interest, because its results were so disastrous. Mrs. Hutchinson had on the voyage been encountered in debate by an emigrant minister, who on his arrival settled at Charlestown. He felt, as all who crossed a lance with her were made to feel, the thrusts of her sharp if not weighty logic. When she applied to the Boston Church for admission this minister came forward, exposed her heresies, and opposes her admission. But Mrs. Hutchinson was full of kindness of heart and good works, especially to those of her own sex who were sick. She soon made her way into the hearts of the people and into the Church.

One of the ministers of the Boston Church at this time was the eminent John Cotton, who came from Boston, England, in compliment to whom the New England metropolis was called Boston. Mr. and Mrs. Hutchinson had lived on their own ample estate near the English Boston, and sat under Cotton's preaching. It was for love of his ministry that they had fol-

lowed him, with her brother-in-law, the Rev.
John Wheelwright, to America.

Mrs. Hutchinson found on her arrival a practice among the brethren of the Church of holding meetings among themselves for the purpose
of repeating and discussing the sermons of their
ministers, Wilson and Cotton, or of whoever
might have the previous Sunday occupied the
pulpit. What more proper, then, than that the
sisters should do the same thing? That Mrs.
Hutchinson should immediately become the
champion of such a meeting, and that it should
become the more popular assembly of the two,
was a matter of course. At times it met twice a
week, and was attended by nearly a hundred
women, among whom were some of the most
prominent matrons of the town. She dealt out
her criticism upon the sermons with an unsparing
hand. Cotton and her brother, Wheelwright,
came out of her ordeal unscathed. In fact, she
pronounced their doctrine the pure gold of truth.
They were "under a covenant of grace." The
most of the other ministers of the colony were
only "so so," or downright heretics, and "under
a covenant of works."

But Mrs. Hutchinson did not content herself

with holding up to her assembled sisterhood (we doubt not many a man crept slyly in) the light of the pastors ; she had a special light of her own to display. The more she pondered upon her own inward spiritual illumination, and the more she held it up to others, the more wonderful it seemed, until it grew in her estimation to a prophetic inspiration. But before her experience had reached this point of consummation her opinions had made great conquests in the seething colony. Let us look a moment at these conquests.

The Governor, when these contentions raged the fiercest, was Henry Vane. He was only twenty-four years of age, and had been in the country but a few months when he was elected over the head of such tried worth and ability as Winthrop. But Vane was the son of a "privy counselor," a scion of an old and great family, and was, moreover, himself a young man of wonderful parts and deep religious aspirations. He was met, when he stepped upon the colonial soil, with profound deference, and his accession to the high office was greeted " by many great shot." The young Governor, thus flatteringly established in power, proved no mere place-

man ; it was just this man whom Mrs. Hutchinson took captive with her sentiments. Cotton
and Wheelwright were standard-bearers in the
pulpit of the same sentiments. Coddington
and Dummer, two eminent magistrates, fell into
line, and all of the Boston membership, it is
said, except five. Wilson, Cotton's colleague,
and Winthrop, a host in himself, were opponents. Most of the country Churches, with
their pastors, were anti-Hutchinsonites. The
reader will see that the conditions were favorable for a first-class quarrel, and such it became. When Wilson, a man who, before men's
blood was heated, was universally venerated,
rose to speak, Mrs. Hutchinson walked out of
church, followed by many of her adherents.
Offensive language was used, and old friends
became alienated. What the precise merit was
of the theological question upon which they
differed it is hard to tell. Perhaps it had no
merit. A conference was called of magistrates
and Pastors " to advise about discovering and
pacifying differences among the Churches in
point of opinion." The discussion which en-
sued was mainly between Governor Vane and
the fiery Hugh Peters, both of whom were des-

tined to figure prominently in the coming stirring scenes of the mother country. Peters gravely corrected the Governor ; Wilson uttered what was termed "a sad speech," for which he " was brought to account " by the Boston Church, lectured sharply by the Governor, and "gravely exhorted" by Cotton.

The General Court, in concurrence with the elders, took the troubles in hand, and appointed a fast for general humiliation and pacification. Wheelwright took occasion on fast-day to denounce the sentiments of his opponents. For this the Court convicted him of sedition. The Governor and the Boston Church interfered in his behalf. The Court showed its resentment by appointing " New Town," now Cambridge, as the place of its next session, and when it met, May, 1637, fiery speeches and sharp management prevailed, quite on the verge of blows, "for some laid hands on others." The old rulers triumphed, and the Boston party went down, carrying Vane and his associates into private life. The combined country vote deposed them, and put Winthrop into office again. Vane soon left the country. A grand synod met in Cambridge to settle differences. They sat three weeks, and considered the opinions which were afloat, and condemned eighty-two of them, which they specified. Cotton joined in the condemnation with little qualification, and may be considered as abandoning the Hutchinsonites from this time. The war against the Pequots raged during the very summer of these later transactions, and the measures of the Government for its prosecution had been crippled by them. But the dissensions seemed tending to abatement, when in the fall and early winter they broke out anew. Wheelwright, whose sentence from the Court was pending, not only adhered to his sentiments and studiously published them, but defied the Court. Certain Boston brethren who had petitioned in his behalf had been understood to intimate in their manifesto that they might resort to arms. Wheelwright was even more offensive, for he threatened to appeal to the king, which amounted to an appeal to the colony's worst enemy, Bishop Laud. Even his own partisans hated the powers over the water, so this was a fatal word to his influence. A sentence of banishment was issued against him. Mrs. Hutchinson was next arraigned, and not only maintained her former sentiments, but laid higher claims to personal inspiration than before. She was sentenced to banishment, but allowed to remain in a friend's house, under watch-care, during the winter weather. She was soon after excluded from the Church by her old friends, Cotton acquiescing, and none objecting, except her two sons.

The signers of the petition in behalf of Wheelwright were now called to a more strict account. A few recanted, and were forgiven. The rest, with other "stirrers of sedition," seventy-five in all, were required forthwith to surrender their arms until they should give proper assurance of loyalty. Some of them were proceeded with "in a Church way," and, for adherence to their alleged errors, excluded.

In the spring the banished ones, and those who felt that the pressure in their old homes was equivalent to banishment, went forth to seek a more congenial resting-place. With these elements thus stirred up and sent forth Roger Williams became immediately associated. Their sentiments, spirit, and conduct must be kept in mind, to understand his spirit and line of service.

The conduct of the Massachusetts Government in their case has been, and will long be,
a subject of discussion and criticism. Its friends
urge that it did but put down sedition; that its
rulers felt that if they did not put down the new
opinions the King and his primate would seize
upon these opinions as a desired pretext to put
them down and stamp out their liberties ; that
they were banished and disarmed not for religious opinions, but for violation of just laws.

Their opposers urge that an unwillingness to
brook dissent underlay all the action of the
rulers ; that the quarrel began and ended in a
difference on religious questions ; and that the
spirit of the Government was seen at Salem
when the Browns were sent home for Episcopal
sympathies, before the pressure upon the colony
from the old country was so keenly felt.

It will be well, before we condemn either
party too unqualifiedly, to ask ourselves whether,
under the provocations of either, we should
have been likely to have behaved any better.
" Man is all vanity."

In the spring of 1638 Mrs. Hutchinson and
her husband, William, who seemed to concede
that she was man enough for them both, turn

up in the cabin of Roger Williams.   Coddington, the eminent magistrate ; John Clarke, a
distinguished physician and good man, were
there, with others of like sympathy.   Why
they were there, and what came of it, we shall
see.

CHAPTER XVI.

FRIENDLY AID GIVEN.

SOME of those whom we have mentioned as in conference with Roger Williams had, on leaving Boston, gone farther north-east for a home ; but, finding the climate too cold, had turned their steps southward, purposing to go to the Delaware Bay. Lodging at Williams' cabin, they found hospitable entertainment, and, as they thought, good counsel. He advised them to remain in his vicinity, and called their attention to Sowams, a little farther down the eastern side of Narragansett Bay from Providence, and to a beautiful island of the bay called Aquedneck.* They were pleased with the suggestion. That there might be no future dispute upon English ownership, Mr. Williams and Mr. Clarke, with two others, visited Plymouth. Its authorities received them with their usual good spirit, told them they claimed

* This name, and, in fact, most of the Indian names, are spelled in many ways.

Sowams as within their judisdiction, but not Aquedneck. To this island, then, the emigrants decided to go. But now came the question of Indian ownership, to dispose of which Williams could do what no other man could. As he had aided willingly the Massachusetts powers in the late war, so now, with an ever ready sympathy with those in trouble, he gives his good offices to those whom they had cast out. The royal owners, Canonicus and Miantonomo, "were very shy and jealous of selling the lands," yet they were willing to bestow them " as a gratuity" upon their loving friends, among the best of whom, of course, was Williams. But they were willing to take a gift, and forty fathoms of white beads were given. Williams obtained from them a deed to make all secure, but the Indians occupying the island had to be induced to leave by further gifts, and so the gift business went on, after the usual Indian requisition, until the colony averred that " though the favor of Mr. Williams had with Miantonomo was the great means of procuring the grants of the lands, yet the purchase had been dearer than of any lands in New England."

Having arranged for the settlement of Aquedneck, the emigrants drew up at Providence a compact which was signed by nineteen of them, seventeen of whom were among those disarmed in Massachusetts. It was a kind of political constitution and Church covenant combined; and as they required all who became citizens to be voted in "by the major part," and to subscribe to the compact, it was not quite so broad a ground as that taken by Roger Williams, who extended his toleration to all, " Jews or Gentiles, Christians or Pagan." The words of the compact are as follows :

"We whose names are underwritten do swear solemnly, in the presence of Jehovah, to incorporate ourselves into a body politic, and as he shall help us, will submit our persons, lives, and estates unto the Lord Jesus Christ, the King of kings and Lord of lords, and to all those most perfect and absolute laws of his given us in his Holy Word of truth, to be guided and judged thereby."

It will be seen that this constitution afforded the broadest Christian toleration, and seems to have been broad enough for all who desired to come.

Aquedneck, upon which they settled, was a

few years later called Rhode Island, or the "Isle of Rhodes." A late writer* traces this name to an early Dutch navigator, who, noticing a red clay about its shores, called it "Roodt Iylant"—the Red Island, which, by an easy transposition, became Rhode Island.

On this beautiful island, later giving name to a State, the emigrants settled. Their town, on its northern shore, they called Portsmouth. They chose Coddington judge, after the Jewish fashion, but soon associated with him three elders. Emigrants came in considerable numbers, and the next spring a part of the first settlers pushed to the southern end of the island, and commenced a new town called Newport. But both towns were considered belonging to one colony.

Mr. and Mrs. Hutchinson and their family removed with these emigrants to Aquedneck. He was honored with office, and died there in 1642. His sons also had office in the settlement, and the more distinguished wife and mother seems to have been content to fall into comparative obscurity. Perhaps she learned, as most warm religious controversialists do,

* Arnold's History of Rhode Island, vol. i, p. 70.

controversy's utter profitlessness. She moved,
after her husband's death, to the neighborhood
of New York, where soon after she and all her
family, except one—sixteen persons—were killed
by the bloody hands of the Indians. The sur-
vivor, a daughter eight years old, was carried
into captivity, in which she lived four years,
when she was recovered and restored to her
friends by the influential interference of the
General Court of Massachusetts.

While the island settlement was getting
started, some people went from Providence to
Pawtuxet river and started a new town. This,
it will be recollected, was a part of the territory
in the original grant to Roger Williams. It
became a great source of disquietude to him
because of the disputes which arose about
titles and jurisdiction. At one time some of its
uneasy citizens invited Massachusetts to rule
over them, and the Boston authorities, thinking,
no doubt, that they needed more ruling, consented to try their hand at it, though they did
not pretend that their charter extended to
them.

But at all times during this early period of
his life at Providence, and in spite of all diver-

sion, Williams was conciliating the relations of
the White people and the Red Men.   Some plain
letters passed between him and Governor Winthrop in 1638, in which the Governor seems to
reflect not only upon the integrity of the Indian
Chiefs, but also upon the wisdom in the management of Williams.   But the latter answers
all complaints in detail.   The Pequots, either
as slaves or as lawless stragglers, committed
outrages on all parties, and made much trouble.
The Mohegans, too, the old enemies of the Narragansetts, now that the common foe, the Pequots, was destroyed, became much suspected,
and their Chief, Uncas, was watched with jealousy.   So hot was the Indian blood getting
that Miantonomo took a guard of over one hundred and fifty men to visit Connecticut, and
confer with his white friends there about the
troubles.   Williams sent him word he would
accompany him, and the Chief waited two days
for him to get ready.   On the way the complaints against the Mohegans grew louder and
more bitter, proclaiming robberies and murder.
One party which they met spoke of six hundred
Mohegans and their confederates as having
plundered large tracts of corn two days before,

and as lying in wait farther toward Hartford to cut off the party of Miantonomo, whom they threatened to boil in a kettle. Things looked squally. The bad news received much confirmation, and Williams' two English companions advised a retreat, in which he, though not easily frightened, joined. But the Indian Chief and his council were plucky. "We are half-way," they said, "and not a man shall turn back." Throwing out guards on every side to prevent surprise, they pushed on and arrived at Hartford safely. They afterward learned that the waylaying party missed them by having expected them two days earlier, according to the time Miantonomo had given out that he should start. So it turned out that Williams' detention of the party, that he might keep the Sabbath at home, had saved them from a bloody collision.

Haynes, the Governor of Connecticut, sent on their arrival for Uncas, that matters might be adjusted. Uncas returned answer that he was lame and could not come. The Governor said this was "a lame" excuse, and sent so urgent a message that the wily Chief came along. Now came the criminations and recriminations of the Narragansetts and Mohegans, the Governor and Williams letting them "give vent and breathing" to their feelings, while they endeavored to ascertain where the truth lay. Seeing that there had been mutual blame, the umpires "drew Miantonomo and Uncas to shake hands," a mode of reconciliation that often proves but a feigning of good-will. On the Narragansett Chief's part there seems to have been a cordial burying of the hatchet, for he twice earnestly invited Uncas and all his men to dine and sup with him on venison which his men had brought in, the Governor and Williams urging him to accept the invitation. But Uncas persistently refused the feast, as he evidently did in heart the reconciliation. The reader will recollect Miantonomo's part in this incident when in the course of this narrative our last word concerning him is told.

When Williams returned, he promptly informed Governor Winthrop of the results of his conciliatory embassy. In this letter is the following, which illustrates Williams' spirit and his style of writing on religious topics:

"Mr. Vane hath written (from England) to Mr. Coddington and others on the island to remove from Boston as speedily as they might,

because some evil was ripening, etc. The most
Holy and Mighty One blast all mischievous buds
and blossoms, and prepare us for tears in the
valley of tears, help you and us to trample on
the dunghill of this present world, and to set
affections and cast anchor above these heavens
and earth, which are reserved for burning!"

In the summer of this year, 1638, occurred
near Providence a shocking murder of an Indian by four White men—runaways from Plymouth. The affair shocked, of course, all the
English, and threw for a time the Indians into
a ferment of revenge. Williams entertained
the murderers immediately after the deed was
done, without of course knowing their character. When the fact came to him, he dispatched
men after them, and ran himself to the woods
to find the murdered man. He was still alive,
but barely able to speak. He gave his dying
testimony, and was carefully nursed for a few
hours and then expired. One of the per-
petrators of this deed, with which "strong
water" had probably something to do, escaped
from Aqueneck in a boat. The other three
were there arrested and sent to Providence, from
whence, by Winthrop's advice, they were sent

to Plymouth. The Pilgrims gave them a fair trial by a jury composed of an equal number of Englishmen and Indians, and they, being found guilty, were hanged.

In September of this year, Williams' eldest son was born, to whom he gave the name of Providence. He was the first English male child born there. The first English female child was born a few months before.

While thus blessed in his domestic relations, and blessing others with his sympathy and aid, Mr. Williams was embarrassed in his financial interest. The source, in part, of this embarrassment was peculiarly trying to his patience when all the circumstances are considered. Some of those at Providence and neighboring settlements who had been banished from Massachusetts, took occasion to write and speak hard things of her rulers. One man had said his hard things in her territory, been called to account for it, and, confessing before the magistrates his error, was freely forgiven. He then left, went to Providence, took back his retraction, and launched his philippics from his safe place at the heads of his old rulers. With their usual thoroughness in dealing with contemners of their authority, Massachusetts proclaimed virtual non-intercourse with Rhode Island. All persons coming from it were arrested, brought before a magistrate and made to swear, on pain of immediate banishment, dissent from such sentiments against their authority, as above expressed. This shut out trade between the settlements, and subjected the Providence people, who had then no ships visiting them, to great inconvenience. Williams often alludes, not in bitterness but sorrow, to this state of things.

CHAPTER XVII.

IMPORTANT CHANGES.

IT is pleasant, in tracing the history of a great
and good man, to turn from wars, great personal crimes, and the weaknesses of Christians,
to matters strictly religious. But, alas, that
weaknesses should so adhere to even great and
good men! It would be pleasant to write, as it
would be agreeable and profitable for the reader
to peruse, a detailed account of the personal
and social religious growth of Providence. But
it was not written at the only time when it could
have been. We are inclined to think that its
good people, including Williams, cultivated their
spiritual life more within themselves than under
other circumstances they would have chosen to
do. Religion is, of course, a matter essentially
between one's own heart and God. But it has
an outward social development. This might
have been restrained in the earlier months, and
even for a year or two, by sharply defined differences of views which had been so magnified

that each adherent felt that on his notions hung
"all the law and the prophets," and the best
part of the Gospel. Then, again, they were
making a desperate struggle for their daily
bread, (this was especially the case with Williams,) for political existence, and as against the
Indians for life itself.

But they had from the beginning Sunday
public worship. We have seen that Williams
detained Miantonomo's expedition to Connecticut two days, that he might keep that holy day.
He was a recognized ordained minister, and
claims in a later controversy with Mr. Cotton
that, notwithstanding all the pressure of other
things, his time had been spent in spiritual
labors "as much as any other's whosoever."
Thomas James, another of the original proprie-
tors, was also an ordained minister. The eccen-
tric Rev. William Blackstone, who came to
Rhode Island two years after Williams, was living only six miles distant, and was known to visit
Providence for religious purposes. Tradition,
which is more reliable on such subjects than
most others, speaks of grove meetings in these
early days, when on pleasant warm Sabbaths
the devout of "all consciences" prayed, sang,

and listened to the Word, under the dome of nature's grand temple.

The first definitely recorded movement toward a Church was in March, 1639, three years after the founding of the colony. It grew out of an act on the part of Williams which our readers will interpret differently, and which, as "soul liberty" is fully recognized now, they may do without contention.

Mr. Williams, on March, 1639, publicly professed his belief that immersion only was baptism. How long he had held this opinion, and by what influences he was led to it, we do not know. Governor Winthrop attributes it to the arguments of a Mrs. Scott, sister to Mrs. Ann Hutchinson. But, however Williams came by his convictions, we may be certain they were his own at last.

Feeling, then, in common with a number of his Christian friends, that he was not baptized, and that he ought to be, the question came, How to secure the ordinance? There was, probably, no minister in any of the colonies who would baptize him. With his customary decision he solved the question. One of his lay brethren, a Mr. Holliman, a man "of gifts and piety," immersed him ; Mr. Williams then immersed Mr. Holliman and ten others. Thus was founded the first Baptist Church in America.

A few months later Mr. Williams made another change, which still more grieved his friends during his life-time, and excites painful regret in the lovers of his memory, and the ad-mirers of the generally noble traits of his char-acter. This change was the no less serious act than that of withdrawing altogether from the visible Christian Church. This, as we shall see, was not in reference to any change of his views concerning his recent baptism as a distinctive question. The fact of this withdrawal is stated by Governor Winthrop, and by Mr. Scott, who was a member of the Church in Providence at the time. The reason they give is, in substance, this : Mr. Williams had come to the conclusion that there could be no authority on earth to gather and organize a Christian Church and to administer its ordinances, except it was derived in an unbroken succession from the Apostles. But the authority is now, he declared, through either the Church of England, which "is an ill authority," or through the Church of Rome, which is Antichrist.   Hence he persuaded himself that the visible Church, with its pastoral office and its ordinances of Baptism and the Lord's Supper, had ceased to exist.   He looked for the speedy overthrow of Rome, and the restoration of a true Church.   These views, stated by others, are confirmed by extracts from his later writings, both epistolary and controversial.   The following letter,* written to Governor Winthrop, of Connecticut, under date of September 10, 1649, throws light upon his views : " At Seekonk a great many have lately concurred with Mr. Jo. Clarke and our Providence men about the point of a new baptism and the manner of dipping ; and Mr. Jo. Clarke hath been there lately, and Mr. Lucar, and hath dipped many.   I believe their practice comes nearer the first practice of our great Founder, Christ Jesus, than any other practices of religion do ; and yet I have not satisfaction, neither in the authority by which it is done, nor in the manner, nor in the prophecies concerning the rising of Christ's kingdom after the desolation by Rome.   It is here said that the Bay hath decreed to prosecute such, and

* Mass. Hist. Col.   4 Series.   Vol. vi, p. 274.

hath writ to Plymouth to prosecute at See-konk."

The old friends of Williams of the Salem Church proceeded to act on his case, and those from that Church who were his fellow-offend-ers. Their exclusion is announced to the other Churches of the Bay in a circular letter signed by the pastor, Hugh Peters, Williams' succes-sor. The reason for the exclusion is given in these words : " These wholly refused to hear the Church, denying it, and all the Churches in the Bay, to be true Churches, and all, except two, are rebaptized."

It is pleasant to be able to state that Mr. Will-iams did not indulge, as his false position made an occasion for him to do, an uncharitable spirit toward those who remained in the Church hon-oring its ministry and upholding its ordinances. He wrote, in 1644 : " Thousands and tens of thousands, yea, the whole generation of the righteous, who, since the falling away from the primitive state or worship, have and do err fundamentally concerning the true matter, constitution, gathering, and governing of the Church ; and yet, far be it from any pious breast to imagine that they are not saved, and that their souls are not bound up in the bundle of eternal life."

There is a relieving circumstance to his false position even better than this. He continued, in happy inconsistency, to virtually preach and labor publicly to win souls to Christ. He believed that the office of "teacher" was not extinct; that is, that a man might be moved by the Holy Ghost to publicly explain and enforce God's word—the essence of the duty of a Gospel minister, we should think. We shall, therefore, find him engaged in the good work of preaching to the Indians, and seeking to publish his sermons as tracts for their spiritual welfare.

CHAPTER XVIII.

SOME SAD THINGS.

THE character of Mr. Williams cannot be understood without following him to some extent in his relations to the stirring events which were going on around him. Unhappily, these events involved great differences between the colonists. They excited bitter altercations at the time, and have been subjects of discussion among historians to this day, who arrive at different conclusions in reference to them. But time and patient investigation is narrowing the divergency of these conclusions. We shall note the events only so far as we deem them indispensable to the appreciation of Williams' conduct and spirit.

That part of Providence which made the village of Pawtuxet on its southern boundary seemed appointed unto contention. First, their boundary line and the rights of its settlers to certain meadows were in dispute. Though they proved themselves abundantly able to carry on a first-class neighborhood quarrel without the help of any new-comer specially gifted in this direction, yet such a one came. His name was Samuel Gorton. He was a puzzle, a wonder, and, to some extent certainly, a pest to the people of his day. He had his admirers, of course, and seems to have had learning, ability, and not a few good social and moral points. The difficulty of a proper estimate of his character is acknowledged at the present time. On coming to the country, in 1637, he went to Plymouth, where he raised a dust of controversy, and was contemptuous, for which, it is said, they whipped him. If the latter fact was true, we are quite sure he behaved badly. He then went to Aquedneck, where, raising another dust, he received permission to leave, and not return. He then went to Providence, enjoyed Williams' hospitable entertainment, agreed with him in his views of liberty of conscience, but excited his disapproval in reference to many other matters, stirred up the Providence people, and settled down at the village of Pawtuxet. Here he was joined by old friends from Aquedneck, with whom he united in so heated a quarrel with the other settlers that the parties came to blows, and some bad blood was shed. His opponents seemed to acknowledge a defeat in this inglo-rious warfare, and appealed to Massachusetts for defense, whose rulers, though they claimed no chartered right to the territory, responded to the appeal, and undertook to right up things at Providence. Foreseeing the rod, Gorton and his friends went across the Pawtuxet river, con-tracted for a site with the chief sachems, and formed what became the town of Warwick. But contention, like a tainted air, followed them. Subordinate chiefs disputed their title, appealed to Massachusetts, before whose author-ities Gorton and his friends were brought by an armed force. If at the hands of the mild, con-siderate Pilgrims Gorton was whipped, he might well tremble now. He was put upon trial for his life, with his ten companions, and escaped, it is said, capital punishment by three votes only. They were kept during the following winter at labor, with a chain bolted to the leg. In the spring they were dismissed with the ad-monition not to trespass upon any Massachu-setts territory nor to return to Warwick on pain of death.

While these painful transactions were going on, Indian troubles were assuming a new aspect. The Indians were fast obtaining possession of fire-arms, and acquiring skill in their use. Dutch and other unprincipled traders had supplied them with muskets and ammunition, and their bearing was considered increasingly insolent. Thus threatened, Massachusetts, Plymouth, Connecticut, entered into a confederation. Its terms were signed May 19, 1643. Its object was, "Mutual help and strength in all future concernment, that as in nation and in religion so in other respects we be and continue one." It was the foreshadowing of the constitutional unity of the North American States. Confederation was to the fathers, as to their children, a tower of strength.

But in this new formed colonial unity, Providence and the Island settlements were left out in the cold. The moral influence of this fact upon the Indians must have been bad, and increased the exposure of the rejected Englishmen to savage hostility. But it is not too much to say that Roger Williams alone was a better defense to his people against Indian wrongs than all the guns of the combined colonies.

The reader will now see, in the movements of
Roger Williams and his friends, the connection
with our story of what has thus far been stated
in this chapter. The danger to their independence threatening them from Massachusetts,
their growing numbers and developing unity of
interest, made Aquedneck and Providence talk
of a political unity. And, as their civil existence was ignored by their neighbors, they began
to move to obtain a charter from the Home
Government. Newport inaugurated the movement in the fall of 1642. The island soon after
united with Providence in sending Roger Williams to England to secure this important object.
Not being permitted to sail from a Massachusetts port, he left for New York about the time
of the formation of the colonial compact, and
was no doubt quickened in the interests of his
missions by the omission from it of his people.
His domestic responsibilities had been increased
by the birth of his fourth child, in July, 1640,
and by that of a second son in February, 1642.
His poverty was still pressing him sorely, and
the expenses of his mission, as we shall learn,
were but loosely guaranteed by his constituents.
Yet he braved all for the common weal. On

arriving at New York—then "Manhattoes"—
he found a cruel war raging between the Dutch
and Indians. It was the one in which Mrs.
Hutchinson and family had been killed. He
interposed his powerful influence, and secured,
for the time at least, a peace. He then embarked on board a Dutch ship for the land of
his fathers and of his youth.

Leaving Williams on the wide ocean, let us
turn to an event which transpired in his absence—one of the saddest in the history of New
England.

The reader has met Miantonomo in Council
with Mr. Williams, in faithful co-operation with
the English in fighting the Pequots, in honored
intercourse with the rulers in Boston, and in the
perilous march from Narragansett to the Connecticut. Whether in Council or in war, he is,
so far as the records show, the discerning, high-
minded, faithful, and energetic friend of the
Whites. A few weeks after Williams left the
country a war occurred between Uncas and
Sequasson, a Sachem on the Connecticut river,
who was on friendly relations with Miantonomo.
Both the parties in the fight appealed to the
English, who in effect replied, You may fight

the quarrel out. Miantonomo took up the cause
of his ally, and, in conformity with a treaty
stipulation of six years before, inquired of the
Governor at Boston if he would be offended
if he made war upon Uncas. The Governor
threw the responsibility back upon the Chief,
telling him that if he had been wronged and
could not get satisfaction he must do as he
thought wise and right. Being relieved, therefore, from the fear of a fire in the rear from the
English, Miantonomo hastened to the field of
action with a thousand men. Uncas was his
old foe, and the enmity thinly covered in the
union of the two tribes against the Pequots
seems to have urged the Narragansett Chief on
with unguarded impetuosity. Uncas met and
defeated his whole force with not more, it is
stated, than four hundred men, proving that
" The battle is not to the strong." Besides defeat, the unfortunate Chief encountered treach-
ery among his own men. Two of his captains
betrayed him into the hands of Uncas. His
subjects offered a large ransom for him, and
claimed afterward that it had been accepted
with a promise of his release. Gorton, to whom
and his friends he had sold Warwick, sent word

to Uncas to deliver up his royal captive to the English at Hartford, threatening him with their vengeance unless he did. Gorton hoped thereby to secure his liberty. Miantonomo was carried to Hartford, and at his own request kept under guard until the meeting of the Commissioners of the United Colonies at Boston the following month. Uncas submitted the disposal of his prisoner to them, and they accepted this gratuitous service. This responsible body of men declared after deliberation that they did not see sufficient grounds for putting him to death, but they did not think that it was safe to set him at liberty. In this perplexity they " called in five of the most judicious Elders and propounded the case to them, and they all agreed that he ought to be put to death." The Commissioners were then ordered to call Uncas on their return to Hartford, and deliver to him the captive Sachem, telling him that he might put him to death as soon as he reached his own territory. The Commissioners, of course, delivered this order. Two Englishmen were sent with Uncas to witness the execution, and to promise him aid if the affair brought down upon him the fury of Miantonomo's friends. No

Williams was not near to throw himself between his old friend and the condemning Elders and Commissioners, and to ward off the murderous arm of Uncas. The sentence was executed in its letter and *spirit*.

It is said in defense of this atrocity that Miantonomo was at the head of a general conspiracy of the Indians against the English; that he had broken his agreement made at Hartford, and that he was turbulent in spirit. But the *Commissioners* did not believe this, for their verdict in effect was, We find in him nothing worthy of death.

To be sure they gave a ready concurrence, as an after-thought, with the sentence of the Elders. It is a noteworthy fact, too, that they consulted only five of the fifty Elders then assembled at Boston in a General Convocation. We may charitably believe, in absence of proof to the contrary, that the remaining forty-five would have given their voice against the condemnation. " From their own account of this affair the English of the United Colonies stand condemned in the trial of time at the bar of history." *

* Samuel G. Drake, in " Biography and History of the Indians of North America." Book II, p. 65.

CHAPTER XIX.

MUCH PLEASANTER MATTERS.

WE left Williams on board a Dutch ship at Manhattoes, about to sail for the father-land. We must not think of him as on board one of our modern sumptuous packet-ships, much less as enjoying the elegant accommodations of an ocean steamer. A Dutch ship then was less comfortable than "a coaster" now, and the voyage to England was no pleasant excursion. We should be interested to know the incidents of this trip made in the summer of 1643 by the Founder of a State. But we doubt whether he thought any body would care to read them. Besides, he had employment in reference to his life-work—the instruction of the Indians.

He had, we have seen, been diligently for fourteen years gathering scraps of information concerning the Indian language. Now, in the ship's cabin, with its disquietudes, he carefully amplifies and arranges them. They grow to a repository of knowledge on the subject, which he publishes immediately on his arrival in London under the title of "A Key into the Language of America ; or, A Help to the Language of the Natives in that part of America called New England." It contained, also, valuable information concerning the Indian tribes, then little known, to all of which were added "Spiritual observations, general and particular." It was dedicated to "well-beloved friends in Old and New England." He says, "The key respects the native language of it, and happily may unlock some rarities concerning the natives themselves. A little key may open a box, where lies a bunch of keys." His desire for the conversion of the Indians, which was ever the burden of his heart, he expresses in the dedication in his own peculiar way: "I am comfortably persuaded that the Father of Spirits who was graciously pleased to persuade Japhet, the Gentile, to dwell in the tents of Shem, the Jew, will in his holy season (I hope approaching) persuade the Gentiles of America to partake of the mercies of Europe; and then shall be fulfilled what is written by the prophet Malachi, that from the rising of the sun—in

Europe—to the going down of the same—in America—my name shall be great among the Gentiles."

The following will answer for examples of his method of "improving" in a pious manner upon the definitions and phrases given in the book. It made a religious tract of his dictionary. "Manit, Manittowock.—God, gods.

Observation. He that questions whether God made the world, the Indians will teach him. I must acknowledge I have received in my converse with them many a confirmation of those two great points, Heb. xi, 6, namely, 1. That God is; 2. That he is a rewarder of them that diligently seek him. They will generally confess that God made all; but them in special, although they deny not that Englishmen's God made Englishmen, and the heavens and earth there; yet their gods made them, and the heavens and the earth where they dwell.

"Nummus quauna—muckqun manit.—God is angry with me. Observation. I heard a poor Indian, lamenting the loss of a child, at break of day call up his wife and children and all about him to lamentation. With abundance of tears he cried out, 'O God, thou hast taken away my child! thou art angry with me! O, turn thine anger from me, and spare the rest of my children."

Not content with his prose comments and reflections on his definitions, Mr. Williams ventures into daring experiments in poesy. The reader will not suspect that he borrowed the following example from one of the old fathers of the poetic gift:

> " Two sorts of men shall naked stand
>   Before the burning ire
> Of Him that shortly shall appear
>   In dreadful flaming fire.
> First, millions know not God, nor for
>   His knowledge care to seek ;
> Millions have knowledge store, but in
>   Obedience are not meek.
> If woe to Indians, where shall Turk,
>   Where shall appear the Jew ?
> O, where shall stand the Christian false ?
>   O, blessed then the true ! "

"The Key" closes in the following devout strain, which is worth many times all its rhyming, and which exhibits in a pleasing light the spirit of its author: "Now to the most high and most holy, immortal, invisible, and only wise God, who alone is Alpha and Omega, the beginning and the ending, the first and the last, who was and is and is to come; by whose gracious assistance and wonderful supportment in so many varieties of hardships and miseries I have had such converse with barbarous nations, and have been mercifully assisted to frame this poor Key, which may through his blessing, in his own holy season, open a door, yea, doors of unknown mercies to us and them, be honor, glory, power, riches, wisdom, goodness, and dominion ascribed by all his, in Christ Jesus to eternity. Amen."

Mr. Williams stepped ashore in London, his manuscript "Key" in hand, and burdened with the responsibilities of his mission, to encounter a whirlwind of political convulsion. The mass of the people were in arms against their infatuated King, Charles I. The fight was yet raging, and the result uncertain. The Parliament, the people's government, had the inside track, holding the reins of power. Henry Vane, recently the young Governor of Massachusetts, who had shared with Williams the confidence of the Indians, was now Sir Henry Vane, and high in authority in the anti-King Charles movement. Williams, whose friendship he shared in New England, became his guest in his aristocratic home. Men in high places had ears more than ever before for Williams' doctrine of religious liberty. The breezes favoring his mission were steadily rising, and he had skill enough to spread his sails to catch them. The House of Commons had passed the previous spring a liberal law in reference to New England commerce, intended to conciliate toward its side of the fight the colonies. Scarcely had Williams become domiciled with his influential friend, before a Council for the Colonies was appointed, with the Earl of Warwick at its head. This, for Williams, was a spanking breeze in the right direction. Sir Henry aided him in getting his craft in good trim, and he was soon laden with a charter for "Providence Plantations in the Narragansett Bay in New England." It associated Portsmouth and Newport on Aquedneck, (now getting to be known as Rhode Island,) and Providence. It gave the English of the Narragansett country, which included these towns, liberty to govern themselves, only requiring that their laws should conform to the laws of England "so far as the nature of the case would admit." His mission ·was a complete success, and with a glad heart he turned his face toward his New England home.

Before accompanying him in his voyage, or joining his townsmen in their welcome, let us pause briefly to notice a singular incident, and what came of it, which concerned Williams' history.

A man during the stirring times preceding his visit lay in Newgate prison "for conscience' sake." His body was closely shut up, but freedom's air poured through his prison grates. He yearned to send a response to the notes that it wafted to him, but his voice could not be heard, and he had neither paper, pen, nor ink. But strong wills find ready ways. His keeper, a woman, brought him milk, in bottles whose stoppers were paper, from a friend in London. On these he wrote in milk an essay on religious freedom. His friend in London, to whom the keeper sent it, read it by the fire and transcribed it. It found its way through the press, and a copy of it floated across the water to the Rev. John Cotton, of Boston, whom we met in the Hutchinson excitement. Mr. Cotton wrote an answer to it. Mr. Williams published, just before he closed his first charter mission, a reply to Cotton under the title of "The Bloody Tenet." He says of the author whom he reviews, "He writes, as love hopes, from godly intentions, hearts, and hands ; yet in a marvelous different style and manner from the arguments against persecution—the arguments against persecution in milk, the answer for it (as I may say) in blood."

Williams's book is written in the form of a dialogue between Truth and Peace. It discusses the question of religious liberty from the point of view taken at the present day by all lovers of freedom. Its arguments are put with spirit, and its style is often beautiful. It opens in this manner :

"Truth. In what dark corner of the world, sweet Peace, are we two met ? How hath this present evil world banished me from all the coasts and quarters of it, and how hath the righteous God, in judgment, taken thee from the earth ? (Rev. vi, 4.)

"Peace. 'Tis lamentably true, blessed Truth, that the foundations of the world have long been out of course. The gates of earth and hell have conspired together to intercept our joyful meeting and our holy kisses. With what a weary, tired wing have I flown over nations, kingdoms, cities, and towns, to find out precious Truth."

This tract called out a reply from Cotton and a rejoinder from Williams, both with quaint titles, and the controversy ran through a number of years. The disputants, to their credit it may be said, dealt in sharp arguments, but kind words.

Williams' heart and head appear well in them, but not better than in the circumstances under which some part of the series was prepared. He was, as we have said, in London. The commotion in the nation had stopped the supply of coal from Newcastle. The poor of the city were mutinous for fuel. Williams received a commission from the Parliament and city to obtain supplies for them. This business brought him into many changes " of rooms and corners," caused much travel, in which he was "in a variety of strange houses, sometimes in the fields, where he was forced to gather and scatter his loose thoughts and papers."

It was fitting that thoughts in such an age on religious liberty should be penned in the midst of labors for the suffering poor.

Mr. Williams landed in Boston in September, 1644. The reader, who saw him embark for England at New York because he was forbidden to visit the soil of Massachusetts, will wonder how he dared to take a return passage for its metropolis. The explanation is this. Several noblemen and others of Parliament gave him a letter addressed to the Governor, assistants, and their friends in general, of Massachusetts. They say they had long noticed " the affections of conscience " of Mr. Williams, and known his sufferings at the hands of the prelates. They speak of his " Key " in highly complimentary terms, and allude to his great and good labors in behalf of the Indians. They inform the Governor and his associates in office that Parliament has given the bearer and his friends "a free and absolute charter of civil government." They say that they view with " sorrowful resenting " " such a distance " between brethren in America who have experienced so many persecutions in common in the Old World and so much trial in the New, and who, at the same time, mutually speak well of each other.

The purport of all this seemed to be, We

think well of you, friends of Massachusetts, and highly also of Williams, and wish you to let him pass unmolested to his Narragansett home ; and this was done.   But the Boston authorities declared at the same time that "upon the examination of their hearts they did not see any reason to regret former proceedings against him, or to change their course in the future, unless he could be brought to lay down "his dangerous principles of separation."

Mr. Williams had a triumphal entrance into Providence.   The citizens met him at Seekonk, and escorted his passage across the river in fourteen canoes, his canoe being " hemmed in in the middle" of them.

He was "home again," and deservedly greeted as a benefactor.

He found, nestled in the midst of his family, a little Joseph, born to him in his absence, and now about nine months old.

CHAPTER XX.

AN OUTLOOK FROM A TRADING-HOUSE.

THE settlements about Narragansett Bay were now, in their rights of self-government, on legal equality with the neighboring colonies. But their work of organization was yet in a very imperfect state. In bringing it into a good working condition they had peculiar difficulties to overcome. The very excellence of their foundation material—the broadest religious liberty—was an occasion of great perplexity in building their political edifice. Their English brethren about them, in common with many other new-comers, gave it many a jostle, and hit it with sharp, disparaging words. It was the stone which other New England builders rejected, though now it is "the head of the corner" in all our political edifices. But the obstacles were not all from without. Their population became for a while in a measure like David's army, when he was endeavoring to secure to himself a God-given authority in opposition to that of Saul. In 1645, when the charter had just come, there were in Providence alone one hundred and one men able to bear arms. But many of these refugees from the religious intolerance of both the Old and parts of the New World insisted that this new foundation-stone was intended for a house in which all were to do as they pleased. They abused the right of religious freedom, as many now abuse the right of a popular vote. The principle in neither case is answerable for the abuse.

The recipients of the new charter did not get their reconstructed ship of state afloat until 1647. Her model was, as we have seen, in one important respect, new. Her builders had little or no precedent for such a construction. The officers and common hands had not well adjusted the question of their relation to each other. It is not strange, therefore, that she sailed at first only tolerably well. The builders of the first steamboat are said to have boasted greatly at her feat of four miles an hour against the current. This new political craft had a strong current, new machinery, and untried hands. We shall be prepared for a charitable judgment concerning her early efforts for success, and appreciate the credit of her ultimate, perfect triumph.

We cannot follow the history of the difficulties between the settlements on the Massachusetts and Narragansett bays. It is one of the most perplexing portions of our colonial history. We shall only glance at it as it crosses the path of Williams.

At the organization of the Government under the charter John Coggeshall was chosen President, and Roger Williams one of the assistants. We naturally expect to see Williams' name connected with the highest office. But, as we shall notice, he had not been remunerated for his expenses in getting the charter. He might have been reluctant to take office under circumstances which compelled the colony soon after to follow Plymouth's example, and fine those who declined it.

These new legislators proceeded to form a code of laws in reference to civil matters only. In reference to religion they add : "Let the lambs of the Most High walk in this colony without molestation, in the name of Jehovah their God, for ever and ever."

One of the first acts of the colony was to

vote Roger Williams a hundred pounds for his trouble and expense in getting their charter. It was assessed upon the three towns—fifty to Newport, thirty to Portsmouth, and twenty to Providence, which shows that the island towns had outstripped in wealth the mother town. This seems a small sum—say five hundred dollars—for three towns to pay. But it came in small installments, and a balance was never paid.

Soon after his return from England Williams removed from Providence further down the eastern shore of Narragansett bay, some distance below the settlement made by Gorton's company. He called the place by its hard Indian name—Cawcawnqussick. It is now North Kingston, by which name we will know it. Here he established a trading-house, purchasing, in connection with it, a landed estate. Very likely a suit of clothes bought the land, and his own strong arm felled and hewed the trees of which the house was built. To have stocked his establishment with goods he must have had credit, for his poverty at this time is repeatedly stated. By special law he was permitted to suffer a native to kill fowl. He was also intrusted by law with a liquor agency. It was one of the first attempts to chain the alcohol demon. He was permitted "to sell a little wine or strong water to some natives in sickness." The terms of sale were stringent, it seems. It was only "a little," "in sickness," and to "some" only at that. But the law was very partial. It let alcohol loose on the White people, who have never been any better able to manage him than Indians. But, in reference to alcohol, our fathers only failed where we have constantly blundered.

While in England, Williams became acquainted with John Winthrop, Jr., son of Governor Winthrop, of Massachusetts. With the father Williams had always been in Christian intimacy, though differing on questions of the times. The son was now Governor of Connecticut, and is known in New England history only less than his distinguished father. The younger Winthrop was early known as a man of learning, genius, and integrity. Roger Williams' residence at North Kingston was relieved by a frequent correspondence with him, and, it would seem, an occasional exchange of visits. The letters which have been preserved range through a great variety of topics, many of them of only a local interest. We shall give so much of those of Williams as illustrates his tastes and principles.

One under date of May, 1647, gives Winthrop, at his request, his correspondent's experience in the use of hay seed. It gives us a peep at the farming of the times, and shows that then, as now, it was a study. The same letter says, concerning Indian affairs, " reports are various ; lies are frequent." We are not surprised at such a statement of " Indian affairs." It might have been preserved until the present time, and applied generally to those perplexed "affairs." Williams gives in close to the young Governor some advice, which is even better worth preserving. He says : "These things you may and must do: 1. Kiss truth where you evidently upon your soul see it. 2. Advance justice, though upon a child's eyes. 3. Seek and make peace, if possible, with all men. 4. Secure your own life from a revengeful, malicious arrow or hatchet. I have been in danger of them, and delivered yet from them ; blessed be His holy name in whom I desire to be.' "

Williams, in a letter a few months later, thanks Winthrop "for the sight of papers from England." The "news" which they contained was, no doubt, at least several months old. This was a long time to wait when a great nation—their fatherland—was being shaken to its foundation. Now Connecticut and Rhode Island may know at noon what King William of Prussia did at sunrise before Paris.

Mr. Williams, in one of his letters, refers to an incident connected with the Indian women. Many complaints had come to him from Connecticut concerning the Indians, in reference to which he was acting in his established character as peace-maker. One of these complaints was that the White women had become afraid of attacks from the Indians. A chief with whom Williams was conferring bid him tell Winthrop that the men of his tribe never did, and never would, meditate the least harm against Mrs. Winthrop or her neighbors; and, still further, that the women of his town would send her a present of corn, if the Governor would appoint some one to receive it.

The peculiar style of Mr. Williams and the characteristic turn of his religious feelings crop out in this correspondence. The following are examples : " The counsels of the Most High are deep concerning us poor grasshoppers, hopping and skipping from branch to twig in this vale of tears."—" Our candle burns out day and night ; we need not hasten its end by swaling (melting and running down) in unnecessary miseries, unless God call us for him to suffer, whose our breath is, and who hath promised to such as hate life for him, an eternal life."

He commences one of his letters in the following strain : " Best salutations presented to you both, with humble desires that since it pleaseth God to hinder your presence this way he may please, for his infinite mercy's sake, in his Son's blood, to further our eternal meeting in the presence of Him who sits upon the throne, and the Lamb forever ; and that the hope thereof may be living, and bring forth the fruits of love where it is possible, and of lamenting for obstructions."

While these letters were passing from Williams to Winthrop, burdened often with efforts to conciliate him, and through him both the Connecticut and Massachusetts colonies, toward the Indians, he had at home his hands and heart full of the work of a peace-maker.

In December, 1647, Williams and other principal men of the colony met to consult on the best method of harmonizing their difference. A paper was drawn up, evidently by Williams, suggesting the ways of seeking peace. It set forth the great blessing of the freedom they enjoyed, and that ingratitude for it was a just cause for its removal by God. It dwells upon the plots at home and abroad to destroy it. It makes devout allusion to " that mighty Providence who had given them unexpected deliverances," and whose defense they might expect " through love, union, and order." They then enter into a covenant, first, in reference to past differences, and agree " that they will not mention nor repeat them in the assembly, but that love shall cover the multitude of them in the grave of oblivion." Second, they renewedly engage to be faithful to their past promises to their town and colony, " abandoning all causeless fears and jealousies of one another." Lastly, they agree to debate calmly and kindly their difference concerning town and colony affairs when they are up for legal action ; to remember,

when they cannot think alike, that " it is better
to suffer an inconvenience than a mischief"—
" better to suffer the loss of some things than
to be totally disunited and bereaved of all rights
and liberties."

This covenant was signed by eight leading
men.   It would have saved some painful pages
of history if all the leaders had in good faith
signed it.   Soon after its date, Mr. Coddington,
just elected President of the new colony, endeavored to get the island of Rhode Island into
the confederacy of the other colonies.   He was
told that the island would be admitted if it submitted to the Plymouth colony, which had sent
one of its magistrates there to demand such
submission.   The Court of Massachusetts about
the same time claimed anew the towns on the
Narragansett Bay below Providence, and then
Connecticut stepped in with a claim a little
further west.   So " Little Rhody " was likely
to grow beautifully less, and have a small show-
ing indeed for its dearly-purchased chartered
rights.

While the contentions among brethren thus
raged, Mr. Williams renews his conciliatory
efforts.   He wrote a letter to the town of Provi-

dence, in which he expresses the feelings of a
burdened heart in language full of tenderness
and earnest entreaty to forbearance and love.
He tells them "it is an honor for men to cease
from strife," and that "the life of love is sweet,
and union as strong as sweet." He further
says : "Since you have been lately pleased to
call me to some public service, my soul hath
been musing how I might bring water to quench,
and not oil or fuel to feed the flame. I am now
humbly bold to beseech you, by all those comforts of earth and heaven which a placable and
peaceful spirit will bring to you, and by those
dreadful alarms and warnings, either amongst
ourselves in deaths and sicknesses, or abroad
in the raging calamities of the sword, death,
and pestilence — I say humbly and earnestly
beseech you to be willing to be pacifiable, willing to be reconcilable, willing to be sociable,
and listen to the following, I hope not unreasonable, motions." He prefaces his "motion" by
these pithy remarks : "To try out matters by
disputes and writings is sometimes endless ;
to try out arguments by arms and swords is
cruel and merciless ; to trouble the State and
Lords of England is most unreasonable, most

chargeable; to trouble our neighbors of other colonies seems neither safe nor honorable." He then suggests that all their differences be referred for final adjustment to a joint committee from all the towns.

This peace effort was well received, and Mr. Williams was put into a prominent position in carrying it out. Such words in such a spirit could not well fall to the ground.

While thus trying to make his life valuable to others, it came near being suddenly brought to a close. He was going to his trading-house down the bay from Providence with a freight of goods in a borrowed canoe, his own not being in repair. His canoe upset, a valuable part of his goods sunk, and he was "snatched by a merciful, some say a miraculous, hand from the jaws of death."

CHAPTER XXI.

IN LONDON, WATCHING AND WAITING.

WE have glanced at the difficulties that beset the position of the Rhode Island colony. The last development of them was Mr. Coddington's effort to connect the island with the government of Massachusetts. Having failed in this, he sailed with his daughter early in 1649 for England. It was not known by his fellow-citizens what project he had in view. On his arrival he found that the civil commotion had progressed to startling results. The King had been beheaded, and the country was being ruled by a Council of State. For a while the officers of Government were too busy with their own pressing concerns to listen to the request of the adventurer from the New World. But Coddington seems to have waited with watchful diligence, for in two years he obtained a hearing. He urged the modest request to have the island of Rhode Island and that of a small island near it committed to his hands ;

at any rate, the result of his mission was authority to govern these islands during life, assisted by a Council of six men, to be named by the people, but subject to his approval or rejection.

With this commission in his pocket he returned to the New World. Of course, the majority of the people rightly considered themselves sold. The territory of the little colony was thus dismembered, and consternation succeeded to confusion. The island towns, Portsmouth and Newport, were soon astir. They appointed one of their foremost men, John Clarke, to go to England, and secure, if possible, the removal of the rule and government of Coddington. Providence and Warwick were also in commotion, and started a subscription to defray the expenses of an agent to accompany Clarke, to obtain the restoration of their charter as it was. Williams was entreated to accept this agency. But his impoverishing experience in foreign missions, and his large family, now consisting of his wife and six children, caused him to hesitate. Besides, his trading-house was yielding him an income of one hundred pounds a year. Five hundred dollars in gold currency was no small sum for those times, and not to be readily relinquished for an uncertain public interest. But with his usual recklessness of his own affairs, when weighed against the common good, he sold his trading-house to support his family in his absence, and sailed for England from Boston, with Mr. Clarke, November, 1651. Having arrived in England, petitioning, watching and waiting became the wearisome duty of the agents. They were confronted with difficulties, needing the nerves of men accustomed to the dangers of the wilds of the western wilderness. England had just plunged into a war with the Dutch, which absorbed for a while the attention of her rulers. Then the other New England colonies had agents and friends face to face with Williams and Clarke, opposing their request. Even Williams' old and kind friend, Winslow, of Plymouth, was among this number. Each party had friends in Court which were played against the other.

There were two men in England at this time occupying foremost places of influence, in whom Williams would necessarily feel much interest, and would be likely to decide the business in which he was engaged. They were Hugh Peters and Sir Henry Vane. We met Vane as the Governor of Massachusetts, in the Hutchinson controversy. The reader will recollect that it was by his influence mainly that Rhode Island obtained her charter. He had opposed the cause of the King, and was now, under the Council of State, the virtual head of the English navy, and launching its thunders against his nation's enemies. Williams again found a frequent resting place in his family, and a powerful right arm in his great influence.

His relation to Peters were of a friendly character, and in one of his letters he speaks of being at his lordly mansion. Peters had been Williams' immediate successor in the Church at Salem after the latter had plunged into the wintry cold of the wilderness. He was afterward one of the ministers of the " Great Meeting-House " in Boston, and trustee of Harvard College. He had, in the Hutchinson wordy fight, chided Vane publicly for disturbing the peace of the Churches. He was the Pastor of the Salem Church when Williams and his friends were excluded for their faith and practice in reference to baptism. He was born the same year that Williams was, graduated at the same University, though at an earlier age, and had given his step-daughter in marriage to his friend and correspondent, Winthrop, of Connecticut. Before Peters went to America he was one of the most popular and successful ministers of England. His biographer says: " It is a fact conceded by all parties that Peters converted many from sin to God, and governed the public mind as much as Whitefield and Wesley and other modern Methodists have done, both in America and Europe, and are doing."

Peters himself says: " I believe above an hundred every week were persuaded from sin to Christ ; there were six or seven thousand hearers."

Peters had been compelled to leave this fruitful field of labor, and bury himself in the New England colonies, on account of his opposition to the King's ideas of ceremonies in worship. He had returned early in the parliamentary war against the King, and was now a chief power in the Government. Though in New England he had given his voice for Williams' banishment, and advised that a letter of excommunication be sent after him, he now grasped his hand in friendly sympathy, and declared to him that he was for liberty of conscience, and preached it.*

It was with such old acquaintances as Winslow, Vane, and Peters, that Williams was brought into intimacy in the discharge of the duties of his mission.

Williams, though yet poor, and serving a poor if not indeed a neglectful constituency, did not depend upon these affluent friends. His industry and self-reliance were, as ever, apparent during his watching and waiting about Parliament. When under financial pressure in New England his strong hands and ready business capacity served his purpose. Now his excellent scholarship became available. He taught Hebrew, Greek, Latin, French, and Dutch, having for his pupils some of the sons of the Parliament men. He was intimately associated at the same time with John Milton, not yet author of Paradise Lost, but now Secretary of the Council of State. Williams taught the Secretary Dutch, and was in return taught languages into which

* Williams to John Cotton, of Plymouth. Proceedings of Mass. Hist. Society, 1855-1858, pp. 113-116.

he had not before delved. The two were in sympathy in politics, which was in those trying times some bond of union.

Mr. Williams, notwithstanding these engagements, kept his pen busily employed. We have anticipated in a previous chapter the continuance of his controversy with Cotton on religious liberty, and his engagements a part of the same time in the interest of the poor of London. In addition to the other works already mentioned, written at this time, was a small treatise with the title, "The Hireling Ministry none of Christ's." It was aimed at the union of the Church and State, and the compelled support of Gospel ministers by taxation. But in it he ventilates freely his peculiar notions which had resulted in his standing apart from all Christian organizations.

While Williams was thus waiting and working, an incident occurred illustrative of his character. From his lodgings in London he addressed a letter to Mrs. Anne Sadlier, daughter of his patron, Sir Edward Coke, now deceased. He glances at his "mighty labors, mighty hazards, mighty sufferings," through which God had carried him "on eagles' wings." He excuses himself from a call upon her at her seat at Stondon, because of "very great business, and very great straits of time," as he was then expecting to soon return to America. He then thus feelingly alludes to her father: "My much honored friend, that man of honor, and wisdom, and piety, your dear father, was often pleased to call me his son ; and truly it was as bitter as death to me when Bishop Laud pursued me out of this land, and my conscience was persuaded against the National Church and ceremonies and Bishop, beyond the conscience of your dear father. I say it was as bitter as death to me when I rode Windsor way, to take ship at Bristow, and saw Stoke House, where the blessed man was ; and I then durst not acquaint him with my conscience and my flight. But how many thousand times since have I had the honorable and precious remembrance of his person, and the life, the writings, the speeches, and the examples of that glorious light. And I may truly say that besides my natural inclination to study and activity, his example, instruction, and encouragement have spurred me on to a more than ordinary industrious and patient course in my whole life hitherto."

Accompanying this letter was a copy of a tract on Experiments of Spiritual Health, which Williams had written while in the American wilderness, and just published. The Lady Sadlier received the letter and book, and answered with dignified coolness that she had given over reading many books, and therefore returned his with thanks. She mentioned some of the old Church standards as her delight, and, as an offset to his remarks in favor of the radical sentiments of the hour, added : " These lights shall be my guide ; I hope they may be yours ; for your new lights that are so much cried up I believe will in conclusion prove but dark lanterns ; therefore I dare not meddle with them." Williams, nothing daunted, wrote again, touching lightly on matters of controversy, and accompanying his letter with a copy of his " Bloody Tenet of Persecution for Cause of Conscience." The lady was shocked at the title and returned it unread, begging him not to trouble her with any more such books, and subscribed herself, " Your Friend, in the Old and Best Way."

Williams writes again, and goes into a detailed, calm, and cogent argument for religious

liberty. She replies sharply, argues for the
"old ways," for "the late King," "Charles, the
martyr of ever blessed memory," and tells
Williams that "none but such a villain" as
himself would have made against him such
"foul and false aspersions." She tells him that
he has "a face of brass, and cannot blush." He
had recommended to her a certain work on his
side of the controversy, which she says she has
read, and adds: "It and you would make a
good fire." She closes by wishing him "in the
place from whence he came."

This spicy correspondence must have convinced Williams, if he needed such convincing,
that to his doctrine of religious freedom he
must expect as bitter opposition from old friends
of the father-land as from the brethren in the
colonies.

After about one year's waiting Mr. Williams
had the satisfaction of sending to his friends at
home the good news that the Council had
"vacated" Coddington's commission, and directed the towns to unite under the charter as
before. While these joyful tidings were yet on
their way, the General Assembly met at Providence, and voted a request to Williams to get

himself appointed Governor of the colony for
one year.   This was officially forwarded to him,
clothed in warm terms of commendation for his
services, and accompanied by strong expressions
of confidence that he would in that time command the respect of the people to their government, and give them a good basis for future
stability.   But the people were not united in
this nor in any other measure, and Williams
had other and very burdensome work on hand.
The interests of the colony, it was thought, required the agents still to remain.   This might
be good for the people, but it was ruinous to
their unpaid but faithful agents.   Williams
wrote to the towns of Providence and Warwick
the next spring, a letter in which his full heart
was poured forth in the following tender words:

"You may please to put my soul's condition
into your souls' cases; remember I am a father
and a husband.   I have longed earnestly to return with the last ship, and with these, and yet
I am not willing to withdraw my shoulders from
the burthen, lest it pinch others, and may fall
heavy upon all, except you are pleased to give
me a discharge.   If you conceive it necessary
for me still to attend to this service, pray you

consider if it be not convenient that my poor
wife be not encouraged to come over to me, and
wait together on the pleasure of God for the end
of this matter. You know how many weights
hang on me, how my own place stands, and how
many reasons I have to cause me to make haste ;
yet I would not lose their estates, peace, and
liberty by leaving hastily. I write to my dear
wife my great desire of her coming while I
stay, yet left it to the freedom of her spirit because of the many dangers ; for truly at present
the seas are dangerous."

Another year passed away with Williams still
in England, and dissensions raging in the colony at home. He felt that the family foes were
becoming more dangerous than the foreign ones,
and, leaving Mr. Clarke in England, he returned
early in the summer of 1654. Provided with a
pass from the Council of free transit at any
time over Massachusetts territory, he landed at
Boston, and was soon in the midst of his family
and cordial friends.

CHAPTER XXII.

WILLIAMS COLONIAL PRESIDENT.

WHEN Mr. Williams returned from England he brought a letter of conciliation to the Rhode Island colony from Sir Henry Vane. It implored the people in the most earnest and Christian spirit to be reconciled to each other, and proceed at once to establish a government in the interest of all, under the charter just confirmed. This letter was by no means unnecessary. Williams' brave spirit was well-nigh crushed by these internal quarrels. He poured out his feelings in a letter to the citizens of Providence, in language of just rebuke and earnest entreaty. He reminded them of his own great sacrifices and labors to establish for them and their children the broadest civil and religious liberty. He tenderly alludes to the unjust return he had received of poverty and reproach. He closes by proposing a plan of reconciliation.

These letters were well received, and in September of the same year, 1654, the towns were once more united, a government was put in operation with Williams at its head as President, and a flag was flung to the breeze with the word "Hope" added to the old device of an anchor.

One of the first official acts of the new President was a long letter to the General Court of Massachusetts in behalf of the Indians. A general war was imminent. But the cloud passed away to reassume at a later day its threatening aspect with much darker shadings.

But peace in the political household was not yet conquered. An indiscreet reformer sent a paper to the town of Providence, in which he maintained "that it was blood-guiltiness and against the rule of the Gospel to execute judgment upon transgressors against the private or public weal." This wild and utterly disorganizing doctrine had, during Mr. Williams' career, been unjustly attributed to him. The present occasion was a favorable one to re-affirm his doctrine of "soul freedom," which he did in a letter to the town. It had "a certain sound," and was about as far ahead of that age as a steamboat would have been puffing down Narragansett Bay for Manhattoes. In reference to the doctrine of the fanatic, above quoted, he says : " That ever I should write or speak a tittle that tends to such an infinite liberty of conscience is a mistake, and that which I have ever abhorred.   To prevent such mistakes, I shall only propose this case : There goes many a ship to sea, with many hundred souls in one ship whose weal and woe is common, and is a true picture of the commonwealth.   It hath fallen out sometimes that both Papists and Protestants, Jews and Turks, may be embarked in one ship ; upon which supposal I affirm that all the liberty of conscience that ever I pleaded for turns upon these two hinges—that none of the Papists, Protestants, Jews, or Turks be forced to come to the ship's prayers or worship, nor compelled from their own particular prayers or worship, if they practice any.   I further add that I never denied that, notwithstanding this liberty, the commander of this ship ought to command the ship's course, yea, and also command that justice, peace, and sobriety be kept and practiced, both among the seamen and all the passengers. If any of the seamen refuse to perform their service, or passengers to pay their freight ; if any refuse to help in person or purse toward the common charge or defense ; if any refuse to obey the common laws of the ship ; if any shall mutiny and rise up against their officers, because all are equal in Christ, and claim, therefore, that there shall be no officers, nor laws, nor punishment—then, I say, the commander may judge, resist, compel, and punish such transgressors according to their deserts."

But the ink was scarcely dry with which Mr. Williams wrote the above, before he was called to defend the true liberty for which he contended against a most powerful opponent. This was William Harris, one of the few who accompanied him from Seekonk in the canoe when a resting place was found at Providence. He had been Assistant Governor, and possessed great force of character and power to attach others to his person and opinions. About this time he raised the cry against " all earthly powers, parliaments, laws, magistrates, prisons, punishments, and rates." He declared his convictions before the whole Colonial Assembly, and closed by avowing his determination to maintain them, if needs be, with his blood. The

Court, thinking this too much liberty, appointed a committee " to deal with him." Soon after a law was passed which provided for the handing over, at their own expense, persons propagating such sentiments, to his Highness Cromwell, and to the Lords of the Council. This law seemed for the time to have a wonderfully convincing power, and Harris soon after " cried up government and magistrates as much as he had cried them down before." But between Williams and this old friend there sprang up an animosity which will have a painful development in the course of our narrative.

The relations of Massachusetts to Rhode Island engaged, of course, much of President Williams' official attention. Late in 1655 he wrote a calm but plain and earnest letter to its General Court. He says that Pawtuxet and Warwick defied the laws of Rhode Island because Massachusetts claimed them as theirs, and that, between two authorities and obeying none, the English and Indians of these towns had become the abhorrence of God and men. In view of this state of things he generously declares that " if not only they, but ourselves and the whole country, by joint consent, were subject to your government, it might be a rich mercy." " Yet as things are," he continues, he desires them to consider whether it is well, by persisting in a claim upon these towns, for Massachusetts " to be the obstructors of all orderly proceedings " among their people.

He next touches upon even a more serious matter. It seems that the Rhode Island colony were not allowed to procure arms and ammunition from Boston. They had been put, in this respect, on the same footing with the Indians. Mr. Clarke, who still remained in England, had, in the summer, sent over four barrels of powder and eight of shot and bullets. But this was a long distance to send in an emergency when the merchants of Boston had enough to sell. The Dutch and lawless Englishmen were supplying the Indians with guns, powder, and shot, and " strong water." The guns gave them the means, and the " strong water " the disposition, to drench the land in blood. They grew daily more insolent, and, knowing that the Rhode Islanders were discarded by the other colonies, threatened to make them their slaves.

Williams holds this subject up in his letter to the Boston Court in glowing language. He tells them that even Indians, though "notorious in lies," can buy powder and guns of them if they only profess subjection, "while ourselves only are devoted to the Indian shambles and massacres." He grieves that so much blood may cry against them in the exposed condition of the men and their families in the Narragansett country, "who may be destroyed like fools and beasts without resistance."

Even Winthrop, of Boston, wrote in his journal that it was "an error in State policy" thus to deny Rhode Island. He puts it upon the ground that "if the Indians should prevail against them, it would be a great advantage to the Indians, and danger to the whole country."

Williams closes his letter with a postscript which, though penned in a quiet way, ought to have made the ears of the Court tingle. He reminds them that in his return from England through Boston he handed to their Governor an order from the Lords of the Council for his unmolested departure. Now, he adds, "I humbly crave the recording of it by yourselves, lest forgetfulness hereafter again put me upon such distresses as God knows I suffered when I last passed through your colony to our native country."

While thus conciliating his neighbors with Christian words, Williams was benefiting them with kindly deeds. He writes to Governor Winthrop, of Connecticut, that Mexham, an Indian chief of the Governor's region, had sent to Providence for its President's mediation. Uncas' son, Winthrop's ally, had stolen a gun from one of Mexham's subjects. The affair, though small, had the seeds of an Indian fight in it, and so Williams begs the Governor to put upon it "his loving eye, as God should give him opportunity." While thus listening to Indian complaints from Connecticut, there comes a " hue and cry" from the Governor at Boston concerning two runaway boys. One of them the President caught and sent back to his home, and sent after the other, who had passed through Providence.

Mr. Williams' letter to the General Court at Boston not securing a change in its policy pleasing to Rhode Island, he wrote to Endicott, then Governor, who invited him to come to Boston. His next letter to the Court has the surprising date of Boston. He is plainly not suffering the "distresses" inflicted on his way to England. It breathes a gratified spirit, and, in reference to the Indian affairs of which he writes, says: "I do cordially promise for myself, and all I can persuade, to study gratitude and faithfulness to your service."

CHAPTER XXIII.

A TERRIBLE COLLISION.

WILLIAMS was President of Rhode Island colony two years, his last official term ending in May, 1657. It had included convulsions at home and threatening gales from the neighboring colonies. We have noticed briefly the home troubles, and we must glance at the breezes from without in order to appreciate his persistent efforts for peace with all, and his consistent maintenance of his principles of religious liberty.

The famous New England Quaker troubles began in Boston in 1656. Their coming had been anticipated, for rumor had flown across the waters, and, with her customary perversions, filled the people's minds with fears concerning them. Old Canonicus was not seized with greater consternation when he received from the Pilgrims the plague, as he supposed, tied up in a snake skin containing gunpowder, than were the Massachusetts authorities when they learned that a vessel had arrived in port with two Quaker women. The arrival found the colony fasting and praying that they might be spared the visitation of the pestilential heresy which such persons propagated. Believing in acting as well as fasting and prayer, they imprisoned the women until the vessel sailed, and then returned them whence they came. The General Court were accustomed to the banishment of heretics, and their experience gave them confidence in this method of getting rid of them. But they had to deal with opposers of different stuff from any with whom they had heretofore come in contact ; yet the Puritans proved sadly equal to the occasion. The prudent and sagacious Winthrop had gone to the rest of the good. The Rev. John Cotton, who, if not always wise in such matters, was not rash and stubborn, had exchanged his labors for the crown. John Endicott was Governor, at whose right hand, as Deputy-Governor, was Bellingham. John Norton was occupying, as teacher, Cotton's pulpit. It is said that the "temper" of the three men was "unfortunate." It is certain that the temper of those they opposed was unfortunate. The stern and honest, though, as all believe now, grievously mistaken, sense of official duty, met the wildest religious fanaticism. The fight could but be serious, and the result, for a while, doubtful. The Quakers were whipped, and gloried in it. They were brought before the Courts, and availed themselves of the opportunity to denounce against the judges the judgments of God. A few of them had an ear clipped, and rejoiced in the mark of suffering for Christ's sake. They were banished, but returned—some were several times banished, but as often returned—though threatened with death. The magistrates threatened death, perhaps, hoping that the threat, as with other heretics, would prevent the occasion of the penalty; and the Quakers, it may be, believed that the Puritans dare not inflict that sentence. If so, neither knew the temper of the other. When the terrible trial of persistency came, neither would give way, for both thought they were doing God service, and several Quakers were hung.

These harsh proceedings met with much popular opposition. The people generally murmured. The poet,* catching the spirit of

* New England Tragedies—LONGFELLOW.

Norton's character, as he urges Endicott to firmness in his bloody work, makes him say :

> " Then let them murmur !
> Truth is resistless ; justice never wavers ;
> The greatest firmness is the greatest mercy ;
> The noble order of the magistracy
> Is by these heretics despised and outraged."
>
> *   *   *   *   *
>
> " My predecessor
> Coped only with the milder heresies
> Of Antinomians and Anabaptists.
>
> *   *   And, as he lay
> On his death-bed, he saw me in his vision
> Ride on a snow-white horse into this town.
> His vision was prophetic ; thus I came ;
> A terror to the impenitent, and Death
> On the pale horse of the Apocalypse
> To all the accursed race of heretics."

The hated and dreaded sect became, of course, more numerous and more fanatical under the goad and halter of the civil power. Men and women, on hearing what was done in Massachusetts to the Quakers, came from England and other far countries, and from the Rhode Island colony even, seeking the martyr's crown. From among its own citizens, too, aspirants arose for the same honor. Scourging and death proved, as they have often done, the promoters of heresy ; the magistrates were brought to a pause, and the Quaker pertinacity triumphed.

The Courts learned, with regard to religious error,

> " That every flame is a loud tongue of fire
> To publish it abroad to all the world
> Louder than tongues of men."

Longfellow, in describing still further these Tragedies, very naturally represents Governor Endicott as regretting the part he took in them, and as claiming at the same time that the Quakers shared, at least, the responsibility for their sufferings.   He makes him say to Bellingham :

> " Speak no more.
> For as I listen to your voice, it seems
> As if the seven Thunders uttered their voices,
> And the dead bodies lay about the streets
> Of the disconsolate city !   Bellingham,
> I did not put those wretched men to death.
> I did but guard the passage with the sword
> Pointed toward them, and they rushed upon it !
> Yet now I would that I had taken no part
> In all that bloody work."

The Commissioners of the United Colonies recommended to each of their Courts severe laws against the Quakers, and all were to some extent drawn into the attempt to rid their territory of them through the civil arm.   But Massachusetts alone proceeded to extreme measures.

The relation of this sad contention, professedly in the interests of religion, to Roger Will-
liams and his colony, may readily be seen. It
was in violation of the principle for which he
contended, and upon which the Rhode Island
government was founded. The example of its
people was a standing rebuke to the other colonies, and the quiet nestling in the Narragansett towns of all the heresiarchs was a perpet-
ual annoyance. Those who fled from the fiery
ordeal at Boston and elsewhere found a safe
refuge in Rhode Island so long as they did not
offend in civil things.

When the prosecutions of the Quakers in the
other colonies had become an established policy, the Commissioners assembled at Boston
wrote to the Court at Providence urging them
to banish all Quakers from their territory; and
to forbid the coming of others. The Rhode
Island Court, with Williams still at its head,
returned in March, 1657, a decisive answer.
They say in effect that freedom in religious
things is the corner-stone of their civil compact ; that it was " the principal ground of their
charter," and " the greatest happiness that men
can enjoy in this world."

The Commissioners urged their request again in the autumn, and in stronger terms. The reply of Rhode Island, re-affirming its position, contains some significant passages bearing upon the questions of religious liberty. The facts alone which they contain should have made the Commissioners change their mode of dealing with the Quakers. The following are some of the passages : "We find that in those places where these people, the Quakers, in this colony are most of all suffered to declare themselves freely, and are only opposed by arguments in discourse, there they least of all desire to come ; and, we are informed, they begin to loathe this place, for that they are not opposed by the civil authority, but with all meekness and patience are suffered to say over their pretended revelations and admonitions ; nor are they like to gain many here to their way. We find that they delight to be persecuted by the civil powers, and when they are so, they gain more by the conceit of their patient suffering than by consent to their pernicious sayings."

This reply did not suit the Commissioners. They proceeded to demand of Rhode Island the required laws against the Quakers, under the penalty of non-intercourse on the part of the other colonies. The lone colony remained firm, and appealed for support in her position to Cromwell and his Honorable Council, through their agent Mr. Clarke, still in England.

But a great crisis was approaching in the affairs of the Mother Country. Cromwell died in the autumn in which the letter to Mr. Clarke was written. His son Richard, who succeeded him, possessed neither the talents nor ambition of his father, and the reins of government soon slipped from his hands. In 1660 royalty was restored in the person of Charles II. He immediately commanded the colonies to refrain from severe inflictions upon the Quakers, and to send them, when offending against the laws, to England for trial. This measure, so far as penalties of death, whipping, and mutilations of the offenders were concerned, agreed with the growing public sentiment of Massachusetts, as well as elsewhere, and was hailed with joy. Fanaticism ventilated itself for a while through its newly acquired freedom in gross improprieties against nature and common sense, and then the "Quakers" subsided into the useful and honored Christian body of Friends as they exist at the present time. The principles of Roger Williams had triumphed. The "Hope" of Rhode Island grew brighter, and her "Anchor" clung steadily to her sure foundation.

CHAPTER XXIV.

VARIOUS MATTERS.

WHILE the Quaker conflict was going on around him, Williams had less serious but truly annoying contentions nearer home. The boundary dispute, an always present one with his colony, was pressed upon him with bitter personalities. It will be recollected that he had purchased in his own name, and as his own property, the land which had become the Providence Plantations. His deed granted him not only these lands in complete ownership, but certain privileges of pasturage for his cattle along the streams beyond them. But some of those who had taken and now owned plantations upon these lands claimed in clear ownership these pasture-lands too. Among the leaders in this unwarrantable claim was William Harris, the able and persistent foe of Williams. Keenly alive, in neighborhood as well as State matters, toward Indians as well as toward Whites, to strict equity, Williams denounced this claim as

going beyond the deed and wronging the natives. Harris to compass his end wrote out
another deed, much in the style of the one
given to Williams by old Canonicus and Miantonomo, but making it express in explicit terms
his interpretation of the first one. To this he
obtained the signatures of the relatives, the
successors in office, of those old Chiefs. It was
a sharp practice, worthy of the tricksters in
business matters of the present age, for, as Williams declared, these later owners did not understand what the import of the deed was which
they signed. Williams reproved the parties
concerned, and they replied: "*Who is Roger
Williams?* We know the Indians as well as
he. We will trust Roger Williams no longer.
We will have our bounds confirmed us under
the Sachems' hands."

Williams adds sadly: "I laid myself down as
a stone in the dust for these after-comers to
step upon, and now they say, 'Who is Roger
Williams?'"

We gladly turn from these unkindnesses to
a letter written about this time, the autumn of
1660, by Williams to his valued friend, Governor
Winthrop, of Connecticut. The first line shows

that the writer was not so far ahead of the age in temperance matters as he was on the question of religious liberty. He writes: "Your loving lines in this cold, dead season were as a cup of your Connecticut cider, or of that western metheglin which you and I have drunk at Bristol together." The cider would do if it was just from the press; but we trust the Governor's "loving lines" were better to the burdened heart of his friend than the Bristol "metheglin."

There is a reference in this letter to a complaint made by Winthrop in his of the old Sachem Uncas, the conqueror of the unfortunate Miantonomo; he hints at a purpose of banishing him and his brother to Long Island. Williams hails the purpose with joy as likely to give "a truce for some good term of years" to Indian hostility in that quarter. But he adds with characteristic emphasis: "How should we expect the streams of blood to stop among the dregs of mankind, when the bloody issues flow so fresh and fearfully among the finest and most refined sons of men and sons of God!" He then alludes tenderly to the sad events of the Old World, and the death of Winthrop's step-

father, Hugh Peters. Peters' history, so far as
it crossed that of Williams, we have sketched.
He had a few months previous to this died upon
the scaffold for his part in the State affairs
under Cromwell. His last moments were those
of Christian triumph. He had, it will be recollected, become Williams' congenial friend, having adopted his views of religious freedom.
Another of Williams' friends, Sir Henry Vane,
died two years later, by the hand of the public
executioner. Well might Williams say, then, in
reference to such times, that "the streams
of blood" should cease among the Whites
before they could among the Indians. His
closing words are worthy of his head and heart:
"The Lord graciously help us to shine in light
and love universal, to all that fear his name,
without the monopoly of the affection to those
of our own persuasion only."

In a letter at a little later date, after referring
again to the civil commotions in the mother
country, and their dreaded consequences to the
colonies, he says: "You know well, sir, that
the first entertainment of a storm at sea is,
Down with the top-sails! The Lord mercifully
help us to lower, and make us truly more and

more low, humble, contented, and thankful for
the least crumbs of mercy."

Williams did not turn to his correspondence
with Winthrop for all the outer comfort that
this period afforded. His faithful friend, and
the faithful, able friend of Rhode Island, John
Clarke, had succeeded in obtaining a charter
for the colony from Charles II. It arrived at
Newport in November, 1663. The people were
jubilant, for the new rulers in England would not
feel bound by that given them under Cromwell.
It was truly a remarkable State constitution for
those times. In petitioning for it through Mr.
Clarke, the Rhode Island people had said to
the King that it was " Much on their hearts to
hold forth a lively experiment that a most flour-
ishing civil State may stand, and best be maintained, and that among the English subjects,
with a full liberty in religious concernments."

In accordance with this request, the following
clause was put into the charter: " No person in
said colony at any time hereafter shall be any
wise molested, punished, disquieted, or called
in question for any differences in opinion in
matters of religion, who do not actually disturb
the civil peace in said colony."

Thus, with all damages repaired from the late political storm which blew across the Atlantic, the ship whose keel Williams had laid commenced a new career.   Her planks were of the old substantial material.   Her flag bore the same motto as when first thrown to the breeze—"Full liberty in religious concernments."   Among her officers for the new voyage was Roger Williams, enrolled as an assistant.

It has been said by high authority, and with seeming truth, that the first thing this new craft did, with her boasting flag flying at her mast-head, was to pour a broadside into the Roman Catholics.   Beautiful consistency! say her accusers.   Where was Roger Williams about that time? asks one.   We don't hear that he made any objection! exclaims another.

The shot which her guns are said to contain was this : "All men among us shall have freedom of conscience, *Roman Catholics only excepted."*   Her records have been carefully examined, and the law of freedom in religious things stands upon them with no such clause.   But it is found that a committee appointed to revise them, at some time later than 1719, thirty years at least after Williams was dead, put the clause into the printed copy without authority. The ship never fired a gun at Roman Catholics, and was never ordered to do so.

But, continue her accusers, this ship did once, with Roger Williams among her officers, fire at the Quakers. No, it is replied; she did, however, in 1665, fire at all persons among her citizens who refused to take the oath of allegiance to Charles II., which he commanded all to take, and some Quakers were hit. But the very next Court so framed the oath that the Quaker conscience was satisfied in taking it, and they were hit no more.

But Roger Williams was assailed in his day with accusations of an opposite character. He says: "We suffer for their sakes, and are accounted their abettors." His enemies declared, in effect: "You take Quakers into your colony, allow them to believe what they please, and you even admit them into your social circles in friendly intercourse; you are, therefore, a believer in Quakerism." This inference wounded Williams. It ought not to have wounded him, for what unreasonable thing will not people say in excited controversy? He should have waited patiently, as he did with regard to most other

accusations, and let time blow away the dust
and show the real facts. But with a weakness
truly human he assailed the Quakers to prove
his own Orthodoxy. We do not mean that he
struck them with his fist, nor that he stirred up
the mob to drive them out of town. He did in
the case no wicked, but, as we think, a very unwise thing. He challenged their leaders to a
public debate. Now who ever knew such a debate on religious questions in which there was
not more bitterness awakened than conviction
in favor of truth produced! George Fox, the
father of the people called Quakers, was then
at Newport, with other able men of the same
belief. Williams drew up a paper denouncing
Quakerism in fourteen propositions. He sent
them to Fox for public debate. The challenge
did not reach Fox until after he had left the
country. Thinking he had run away to avoid
debate, Williams exclaims : "The Fox has slyly
departed." But, if so, he left able friends who
accepted the challenge. The place agreed upon
was the Quaker meeting-house at Newport.
Williams, though seventy-three years of age,
rowed a boat from Providence to Newport—
thirty miles—in July, in order to engage in the

combat. He arrived there at midnight, before the morning of the meeting, weary and sick. He opened the debate with a few conciliatory remarks, disclaiming unkind feeling toward those he opposed, and disowning pride or vanity in the challenge, but claiming a desire to further the truth and honor God. We may allow the purity of his motives. There was no moderator. A crowd had gathered, of course, to witness the contest. Williams was opposed by three men, two of whom, he allowed, were able and fair debaters. The other, he says, was a wrangler, and, of course, this one had the most to say. The debate went on for three days, seven points were discussed, and the meeting adjourned to Providence. Here it was continued one day, and then broke up.

The immediate results of this affair were great physical prostration on the part of Williams, and a seven days' buzzing in the colony on the merits of the questions and parties concerned. One of the more remote results was a large printed volume by Williams, entitled "George Fox digged out of his Burrowes." The title is a pun on the names of his opponents. Burroughs was a friend of Fox. The

two had jointly written a book on their opinions. Fox and Burnyeat—the latter one of the
debaters—wrote a reply, entitled, "The New
England Fire-brand Quenched." Williams'
friends allow that he appears less favorably as
a Christian in this book against the Quakers
than in any other he wrote. The answer to
him is said to be "coarse and bitter."

CHAPTER XXV.

THE WAR-PATH.

THOUGH Williams was now at that age of life which disposes to retirement and quiet, yet one more terrific commotion went on under his eyes. We have seen intimations in his letters to Governor Winthrop, of Connecticut, that he was alarmed at the bearing of the Indians toward the English. He wished Uncas sent to Long Island. He earnestly studied with them the things which made for peace. He had been a mediator between his brethren and the Red Men for forty years. He must have felt the necessity a painful one to take the sword at last against these wild men whom he had sought to tame by the Gospel of Christ. But he had this consolation, that the war spirit which was now spreading over all New England had not been provoked by himself personally, nor through the indirect influence of a policy he had advocated. If war came to his cabin door, compelling him to bring his gun to bear upon the savage foe to save his own and his children's lives, that foe came not to avenge wrongs he had inflicted.

Two facts of prominence in the war of which we are about to speak must have made it especially painful to Roger Williams. They were these: The tribes most deeply involved in it were the Wampanoags and Narragansetts—the people of his old friends Massasoit, Sachem of the former, and Canonicus and Miantonomo, Sachems of the latter. From these people and their departed Chiefs he had, in the times of his necessities, when his own had cast him out, received home and country. The second fact was that the two most powerful leaders against the Whites were the sons of these old friends. Metacomet, or Philip, as the English called him, was the second son of Massasoit; and Canonchet, of the Narragansetts, was son of Miantonomo. Williams must have seen and known well these Chiefs when they were children in their fathers' wigwams. Upon their heads, doubtless, he had laid his hands, and given them his Christian blessings. He had spoken in their hearing the great truths of the Gospel, and hoped for their salvation.

We shall notice the facts of this war—King Philip's War, as it is called—only briefly, and mainly as it was connected immediately with Williams and with these two noted friends of his.

The indirect cause, or one of the principal prompters, of this war, is generally thought to be the treatment which Wamsutta, Philip's older brother, received at the hands of the Plymouth colony. Massasoit died early in 1662. Wamsutta succeeded his father in the chieftainship of the tribe, and died in a few months. Two eminent historians of his day attribute his death to harsh treatment from the Plymouth authorities. This an eminent Plymouth contemporary denied. We cannot tell certainly the exact facts, but it seems that Philip thought the forty years of his father's faithful adherence to the Whites, and his brother's endeavor to walk in his parent's steps in this respect, were poorly requited by the pale faces. Besides, Weetamoo, the widow of Wamsutta, and a daughter of a neighboring chief, a woman of strong will and great influence, insisted that the English had poisoned her husband. Her influence over Philip is thought to have been potent. The bearing of Philip was independent, and to the Plymouth men he seemed haughty and rebellious. Their tempers were evidently not congenial. He was watched closely, and brought to an account for his conduct much oftener than suited his royal humor. In 1667 he was summoned to answer to a charge of wishing to join the Dutch and French against the English. He protested his innocence, and readily gave up his fire-arms as a guarantee of good will. So well convinced were the Court of his sincerity that at their next session they restored his guns. Four years passed away, and Plymouth was again alarmed. A meeting was held at Taunton between Philip and his chief men and his complainants, before three Boston men as umpires. All the decisions went against Philip. He made confessions, renewed old treaties, and gave up his guns. These were not returned this time, but a short time after the Court at Plymouth distributed them among the towns. For several years Philip had been required to pay a moneyed tax, and also one of " wolves' heads," as an offset to the expense attending the troubles he was accused of making. It is a fact worth noting that Gookin, the superintendent of the religious instruction of the Indians at this time, resented this treatment by Plymouth of Philip. Gookin was a man of some prominence, and then lived at Cambridge. He wrote some sharp letters to the Governor of Plymouth, telling him that his people too severely pressed the Indians. The Governor retorted that Gookin, as a missionary to the Indians, countenanced them in being troublesome. So it seems that the English settlers of those days were not agreed in these measures with Philip.

A few months later Plymouth again summoned Philip to answer for renewed short-comings. Instead of going to that place he went to Boston and complained of these interferences. The excellence of his cause, or the eloquence of his tongue, or both, obtained for him a favorable hearing with certain influential persons, who, after correspondence with Plymouth, went there, accompanied by Philip and his counselors, to bring about a reconciliation. As usual, the savage was found to blame, and more humiliation on his part was the penalty. But it was plainly a constrained humility. The savage in the Chieftain was getting the mastery of prudence, but still he kept up tolerably fair appearances for three years longer. It has been thought that they were years of diligent preparation, and far-reaching plans to exterminate the Whites. He has been credited with comprehending the sacred rights of himself and people in their soil, their country, and their homes, and with seeing that now, while the strangers were few and the Indians many, was the time to strike a decisive blow for freedom. The Narragansetts, the ancient enemies of his people, had been brought into more friendly relations by their mutual connection with Roger Williams. The Indians had possessed themselves of fire-arms, and become expert in their use. The chafed spirit of the haughty Chief grew hot as he saw the means of independence and revenge within his reach. Just before the war broke out, the Governor of Massachusetts sent a messenger to him to demand why he purposed to make war upon the English. Philip replied proudly : " Your Governor is but a subject of King Charles, of England. I shall not treat with a subject. I shall treat of peace only with the King, my brother. When he comes I am ready."

All now, 1674, saw the war cloud hanging over them, and watched anxiously for the place and manner of its first shower of blood. They did not wait long. In the latter part of that year Sassamon, a friendly Indian, informed Plymouth that Philip was entertaining strange Indians, and binding into treaties against the English all the tribes. Sassamon was a way-ward subject of the educational and religious privileges of Cambridge College. He had been a school-master at Natick, then a secretary to Philip, and, later, a preacher of the Gospel. The Sachem went to Plymouth, denied the charges, returned home, and soon after Sassamon was murdered. The Plymouth Court arrested, tried, convicted, and put to death three of Philip's subjects on the charge of murdering Sassamon. Philip intended another year's preparation, but he could not restrain his young men. The first flash from the darkened sky fell at Swanzey on a Fast day, and English blood was shed. It was said that Philip wept on hearing the fact, for the Indians believed that the party in the fight who shed the first blood would be defeated. But the die was cast. The Indian war whoop startled the midnight slumbers of the colonists in every direction, and the gun, scalping-knife, and flames did their horrid work.   Of course, the colonists were soon astir, and the White and Red man were matched in reckless bravery and relentless cruelty.   The deeds that were done on the Indian side are recorded in history in the name of Philip.   It is said that Philip surprised such a party of his enemies, and burned this and that town through a wide extent of country.   Yet it is a singular fact that he was seldom seen in battle, nor could his place of personal operations be often ascertained with certainty.   It was then believed, and is generally credited now, that his master-mind pervaded all the movements of the savage foes.

Rhode Island was not immediately drawn into the conflict.   She had been at peace with the natives.   But as the war raged her territory was invaded, and her people were killed.   Roger Williams wrote early in the conflict to the Governor of Massachusetts, giving prompt information of the movements of the enemy.   By his promptings Providence made some efforts at fortifying the town.   He accepted in his old age a captain's commission, drew his sword, and drilled the young recruits.

The Indians received their first serious blow in December, 1675. Philip, with the flower of his army, had gone into winter-quarters on the western shore of the Narragansett Bay, at what is now South Kingston. He had selected an island in the midst of a swamp and strongly fortified it. But the colonists under General Winslow, of Plymouth, took the fort after the most desperate fighting on both sides. The loss of life was very great, and the sufferings and deaths from the cold and winter exposures were shocking. It is not certain that Philip was at this fight, though the presence of a superior mind was apparent. Some give the credit, in part at least, of the brave defense of the fort to Canonchet, the Narragansett Sachem. Let us turn our attention for a moment to his movements.

The Indians at the bloody fight in December were defeated but not beaten. They left during the winter their bloody footsteps at Lancaster, Mendon, and Weymouth, startling the Bostonians by their audacity and success. They appeared in Rhode Island, and boldly desolated the English settlements from the Narragansett Bay to New London. To divert them from ravages quite too near them, the Plymouth authorities sent out Captain Peirce, of Scituate, with fifty Englishmen and twenty friendly Indians. He marched to a place on the Pawtucket, now the Blackstone river, about seven miles above Providence. Canonchet was there with about three hundred warriors. He was on his way to the Plymouth towns. He had become aware of Peirce's approach, and laid a snare for him into which he most unfortunately marched.

Seeing a party of Indians fleeing across the river, as he supposed to escape him, he gave chase. When his men reached the opposite, or western side, Canonchet and his men rushed upon them with great fury. Seeing themselves outnumbered and likely to be overpowered, Peirce's men turned their faces to recross the river. But up started on the eastern side an ambushment of Canonchet's forces, placed there to cut off their retreat. Thus hemmed in, the brave Captain arranged his men in two ranks, back to back, and sold their lives as dearly as possible. Only one White man escaped, and this was effected in a singular way by the keen wit of one of the friendly Indians. Seeing the

Englishman running, and knowing that he would be overtaken if pursued, he raised his tomahawk and gave chase. He was mistaken for a Narragansett, and honorably left to the capture of his supposed foe.

One of the friendly Indians escaped in an equally cunning manner. Being sorely pressed by an armed, swift-footed Narragansett, he slipped behind a rock. Each was now prepared for the other with a loaded gun. The pursuer waited for the skulker to leave his hiding-place, ready to send a ball through him as soon as seen. Thus the case stood when the man behind the rock slowly raised his cap, placed on the end of his gun, above the top of the rock. Whiz, came a bullet through the innocent cap, and away flew its owner before the cheated Narragansett could reload !

Canonchet's victory was complete. But his success, as it has often been with the world's greatest commanders, proved his ruin. He encamped near the battle ground on the bank of the river. His men were carelessly resting on their laurels, although their Chief had commanded a vigilant watch from the top of a hill. Thus situated, he was surprised about a week

after the victory by four companies of Connecticut volunteers. The panic of Canonchet's
men was complete. Their Chief attempted to
escape by running along the bank of the river,
and, as he attempted to cross, his foot slipped,
plunging his gun under water. His pursuers
were close upon him, and he surrendered with
dignity. The first Englishman who came up
was a young man, who commenced with famil-
iarity to question the Sachem. A look of dis-
dain was the only answer given for some time.
The young man persisting, Canonchet replied
in broken English: "You much child! No
understand matters of war! Let your Chief
come ; him I will answer!"

Joy spread through New England at the capture of Canonchet, for, next to Philip, he was
the most feared by the colonists of all their
Indian foes. He was offered his life if he would
obtain the submission of his people, but he
scorned the bribe. In the early days of the
war, before the Narragansetts had gone over to
Philip's side, he was requested by the English
to deliver over to them such of Philip's men as
fell into his hands. His reply was : "I will not
deliver up a Wampanoag, nor a paring of a

Wampanoag's nail!" When reminded of this in his captivity, he replied: "Others were as forward for the war as myself, and I desire to hear no more about it."

He was carried to Stonington, and soon after shot. When told he must die, he replied calmly: "I like it well. I shall die before my heart is soft, or I have said any thing unworthy of myself."

The desolating sweep of the war reached Providence. It was attacked three days after the victory of Canonchet, of which we have just spoken. As that took place only about seven miles from Providence, the attack was, perhaps, by a raid of his men. Twenty-nine houses were burned, among which was that of the Town-clerk. To save his records he threw them into a mill-pond, from which they were recovered in a damaged state.

Most of the inhabitants had removed to Newport when the raid was made, among whom was Williams' family. But he himself remained, and, seeing the Indians coming, he took his staff and met them on a hill which overlooked the town. He declared to the leaders the uselessness of the war on their part. "You may kill," he said, "the thousands the colonists can send against you, and the King of England will supply their places as fast as they fall."

"Well," said the Chief, "let them come. We are ready for them. But as for you, Brother Williams, you are a good man. You have been kind to us many years. Not a hair of your head shall be touched."

Philip's death closed the war. The death of his right hand, the brave Canonchet, and defeat every-where, drove him to his familiar haunts about the home of his boyhood. His wife and only son, nine years old, were captives among his enemies. His people had been conquered, and, true to the spirit in which he commenced the war, he declared that he did not wish to survive his nation. He disdained to sue for peace. One of his followers advising it, he slew him. A brother of this man, whose name was Alderman, in revenge for his death deserted Philip, and led the English captain to his hiding-place in a swamp. Philip was taken by surprise, and, in attempting to escape, was shot through the heart by Alderman, and "fell upon his face in the mud and water, with his gun under him."

" Even that he lived is for his conqueror's tongue ;
By foes alone his death song must be sung;
    No chronicles but theirs shall tell
        His mournful doom to future times ;
    May these upon his virtues dwell,
        And in his fate forget his crimes."—SPRAGUE.

With the fall of Philip the power of the Indians in New England was forever paralyzed. But the victory cost the colonists a great price. The expenditure of blood and treasure was immense for their means, and their songs of triumph were mingled with bitter lamentations, for bereavement had come to nearly every house.

The close of this Indian war connects with Roger Williams in his appointment on a committee to dispose of certain Indian captives. The town had voted to apprentice them for a term of years, and this committee was to carry out the provisions of the law for that purpose. The longest term of service required in any case was that of children five years old and younger, who were to be free at thirty. The number of years' service lessened as the age increased, and all who were adults at the commencement of their servitude were to go out free in seven years.

CHAPTER XXVI.

THE SUNSET OF LIFE.

WE have seen that Williams bore far into the evening of life his part, and more than his part, of the burdens of State affairs. It would be pleasant could we record that his last days had been blest by a truce in religious controversies. But besides the Quaker controversy, sparks from the ashes of earlier fires of this kind were stirred up and blown in his face. It will be gratifying, however, to note the continuance of the Christian patience and the spirit of forgiveness which adorned his earlier years, causing him to rise superior to all provocations.

This will be seen in the following sentences, taken from an answer, in 1779, to a letter by a neighbor about taxes, in which railing accusations had been made. "I thank you that you have so far regarded my lines as to return me your thoughts ; whether sweet or sour, I do not desire to mind. I humbly hope that as you shall not find me self-conceited nor self-seeking,

so, as to others, not a busy-body, as you insinu-
ate. My study is to be swift to hear, and slow to
speak." This was the soft answer which turns
away wrath. He was yet true to the spirit
which extorted, many years before, this compliment from Governor Winthrop, of Massachusetts : " Sir, we have often tried your patience,
but could never conquer it."

A severer test of the excellent graces of
which we have spoken was inflicted upon him
in a letter* written in 1671 by the Rev. John
Cotton, of Plymouth. Mr. Cotton was a son
of the eminent John Cotton, with whom Mr.
Williams had the controversy on the Bloody
Tenets. The father had in a Christian spirit
confined his denunciations to what he considered Mr. Williams' errors. The son looks over
the pages of the books which contained the
records of Williams' part of the contest, and
revives the war by shooting his arrows at Williams' personal character, imputing to him, if he
is rightly quoted, " the odious crimes of blas-
phemies, reproaches, slanders, and idolatries,"
telling him he was " in the devil's kingdom, a
graceless man, etc." Williams says, " All this

* Proceedings of Mass. Hist. Soc., 1855-57. Pp. 313-316.

without any Scripture, reason, or argument, which might enlighten my conscience as to my error or offense to God or your dear father;" and he adds, " I have now much above fifty years humbly and earnestly begged of God to make me as vile as a dead dog in my own eyes, so that I might not fear what men shall falsely say or cruelly do against me; and I have had long experience of his merciful answer to me in men's false charges and cruelties against me to this very hour." He further replies: "My great offense, as you so often repeat, is my wrong to your dear father—your glorified father. But the truth is, the love and honor which I have always shown, in speech and writing, to that excellently learned and holy man, your father, have been so great that I have been censured by divers for it. God knows that for God's sake I tenderly loved and honored his person—as I did the persons of the magistrates, ministers, and members whom I knew in Old England, and knew their upright aims and great self-denials to enjoy more of God in this wilderness; and I have therefore desired to waive all personal failings, and rather mention their beauties, to prevent the insultings of the Papists or profane Protestants who used to scoff at the weaknesses, yea, and at the divisions, of those they used to brand for Puritans. The holy eye of God hath seen this the cause why I have not said nor writ what abundantly I could have done, but have rather chose to bear all censures, losses, and hardships."

Concerning the book of which Mr. Cotton complains, he asks : " What is there in this book but presses holiness of heart, holiness of life, holiness of worship, and pity to poor sinners, and patience toward them while they break not the civil peace ? " And he adds in an earnest tone : " Sir, as before and formerly, I declare that if yourself, or any in public and private, show me any failing against God or your father in that book, you shall find me diligent and faithful in weighing, and in confessing or replying, in love and meekness."

While thus repelling attacks upon his character, his pen never faltered in seeking to secure redress for the wronged, or alleviation for the suffering.

Richard Smith was a friend of Williams' early manhood, who "for conscience' sake," after various perils among brethren, had settled in the

Narragansett country.   Here, " at great charge
and hazard," he put up " in the thickest of the
barbarians " the first English house ; forty years
after this, in this same house, " with much se-
renity of soul and comfort, he yielded up his
spirit to God, the Father of spirits, in peace."
His son Richard was living on and enjoying
this paternal estate when King Philip's War
broke out.   At the command of General Winslow, Smith then gave " himself in person, his
housing, goods, corn, provisions, and cattle for
a garrison and supply for the whole army of
New England."   It seems that Smith was now
impoverished and neglected.   Thus situated he
found in the pen (though held by fingers eighty
years old) of his father's friend an eloquent
pleader.   The letter has the old ring, and shows
that though the writer's hands might tremble,
his heart was young.

We have stated in another place that, though
Williams could see no truly apostolic Church
and ministry, and so left the Church as now
constituted, he continued to preach and to labor
for the conversion of men.   In 1782, when
eighty-three years of age, he indulged a desire
to publish the discourses he had delivered, as

he says, "to the scattered English at Narragansett before the war and since." He recalled
and arranged them at his fireside. He says of
himself while making an effort to carry out this
purpose, "I am old, and weak, and bruised."
He was, besides, poor. His wealth, as we have
seen, and his golden chances to become rich,
had been sacrificed to the public good. We
learn from a letter of one of his sons, written
after his father's death, that he was dependent,
in part at least, upon his children. To carry
out, then, his benevolent purpose with regard to
his discourses, he was compelled to write to
his friends in Massachusetts, Connecticut, and
Plymouth, as well as those of his own colony.
He assures them that there is in the sermons
no controversy, "only an endeavor of a particular match of each poor sinner to his Maker."
He says, in his letter to Governor Bradstreet,
of Massachusetts, that "those who have a shil-
ling, and a heart to countenance such a soul
work, may trust the Great Paymaster for a hundred to one in this life."

Thus was the ruling passion of Roger Williams' life—a desire to do good—strong when
the weary wheels of nature were about to stand

still. By the preceding sketches we are permitted to glance at the venerable man of eighty-
four years. He sits by the fireside of his humble home, surrounded by his kind children, and
the affectionate wife of his youth. That his
domestic relations were happy, the reader may
be assured by recalling the tender expressions
of his letters from England respecting his wife.
It appears also in the letter he wrote to her in
the wilderness, called " Experiments of Spiritual
Life," etc., in which occurs this passage. It is
strongly figurative, of course, his " posey " being
the cluster of truths he sends concerning the
improvement of his family's religious life : " I
send thee, though in winter, an handful of flow-
ers made up in a little posey for thy dear self
and our dear children to look and smell on,
when I, as the grass of the field, shall be gone
and withered."

Roger Williams died early in the year 1683,
in the eighty-fourth year of his age. The colony which he had founded bestowed upon his
funeral service all the honors and solemnities
of its small resources, and no doubt devout
men carried him to his burial, and made great
lamentation over him.

Through the smoke of the controversial bat-
tles in which Roger Williams was engaged
through all of his eventful life, his faults have
been magnified and his virtues disparaged. But
as the peace-bringing light of a better age falls
upon this smoke and dissipates it, his faults are
seen—though sharply defined—to lie upon the
surface of his character, and divine grace, in-
grafted upon a generously impulsive heart and
a gifted intellect, to be the solid foundation of
it. Though there never have been wanting
those who saw and published his faults, every
generation has borne men of historic note who
have declared their convictions in glowing
language, of the world's great indebtedness to
Roger Williams for his clear conception, forci-
ble statement, and consistent maintenance of
the true principles of religious freedom ; and
no age has contained so many such testi-
monies as our own. But the civil institutions of nearly an entire continent have
their secure foundation upon Roger Williams' principles of "soul liberty." The people of the Old World are reconstructing
theirs upon the same firm basis. These proclaim his fame with more than a trumpet

tongue.   They increase and perpetuate it more than golden statues or marble monuments could do.

We invite the reader to a sight of the mementoes of his history.

Intended Monument to Roger Williams at Providence.

CHAPTER XXVII.

MEMENTOES.

WE trust that the acquaintance that these pages have given the readers with Roger Williams will make them interested in whatever mementoes we may be able to exhibit. We make no extra charge for a walk through our museum, though it has cost us some pains-taking. If you, reader, do not like our curi-osities, you can pass rapidly on; if you are interested, you can pause and do your own moralizing.

We have been at Salem, Mass., often enough during our story to know what connection it has with it. We shall enter it in the railroad cars, and not, as we suppose Roger Williams did, on horseback. Walking out of the front of the depot, and taking the sidewalk on the right hand of the railroad track, and going a few rods until we reach the corner of Washing-ton and Essex streets, we stand directly in front of a brick church. Its marble tablets tell us that it is the First Church, on the site of the first house of worship built in the Massachusetts colony. The society, gathered in 1629, have worshiped on this spot ever since. Here Williams preached. The parsonage was near the church, on a spot covered now by the Merchants' Reading Room.

But by passing along we may stand within the frame, and look upon the oaken timbers of the very church in which he preached. Turning to the right into Essex-street, and walking a few moments, we reach Plummer Hall, on the left hand. Stepping in and getting a queer looking key, one of the fathers of its kind, which will be kindly loaned us, and going into the rear of the building, we unlock the door and enter The Old Roger Williams Church. The reader will recollect our account of the building and dedication of this house, contained in the fifth chapter. There are evidences now of the peculiar plaster and mortar which originally covered the walls and beams. We may imagine the rough, uncushioned seats on which the worshipers sat. What a contrast to Hugh Peters, Williams' immediate successor, this house must have been to that of St. Sepulchre's in London, with its weeping thousands, and many hundreds who had just passed, under his ministry, from death to life!

The room is now stored with many mementoes of the past. The first communion table will connect us with Williams at moments of the most sacred character. Chairs of the antique pattern carry us back to the home circle gathered about the blazing fire of the huge old fire-places. The spinning-wheel speaks of the music Williams heard in his pastoral calls. The old portraits which look down upon us from the walls are those of some of the early fathers.

This house, besides being honored with the presence as worshipers, either stated or occasional, of nearly all the historic persons of the colonial period, was the place where the colonial government held some of its early meetings; they used it too for a watch-house.

After being doubled in size, and, as years passed on, abandoned as a church, and the old and new parts separated, this, the original old church, was used for a school-house, and later for more menial purposes. Finally, its identity being well established, the Salem Athenæum removed it to this place.

Leaving the old church, with its impressive associations, and returning along Essex-street, across Washington-street, to the corner of Essex and North streets, we stand before the Roger Williams House. We give a picture of it as it is now. Its history has been carefully and thoroughly examined by W. P. Upham, Esq., and its identity seems to be fully ascertained.* It has long been known as the Witch House, but its connection with any witchcraft proceedings has never been proved, unless the mere fact that it was owned and occupied by one of the judges of the alleged witches in the great witchcraft furor of 1692 constitutes such connection. It has undergone important changes since 1636, when Roger Williams left his home and family and plunged into the wilderness. That end seen at the end of the picture which has a projecting upper story remains essentially as in Williams' day. The bricks covered with clay, with which its sides were originally filled, still remain, giving evidence that there was then no plastering nor ceiling. Two stout hewn timbers of sound oak cross the rooms of this end. The house, as built by

* See Essex Bulletin for April, 1870.

Roger W   ams' House.

Williams, must have been one of the most capacious and desirable, both as to structure and location, of any of its times. He speaks in one of his letters of selling his house in Salem to pay the expense of the impoverishing consequences of his banishment. From Salem to Providence is a small affair in the way of a journey, taken in these days of steam and railroads. We have seen that it meant something to Roger Williams, taken afoot, in a stormy winter, through a pathless forest. If the reader please, we will start from the very room, the one we have just examined, that Williams started from, and visit the spot on which he finally settled, and where his dust is entombed. We need not avoid Boston, as he did, but shall find it very convenient and pleasant to take it in our way. We know of no foot-prints there of Williams. But the Boston libraries have carefully gathered all the important records, and even the little scraps of information, from recently discovered manuscripts, which throw light upon his life. These have an honored place with like records of the great and good men who saw not eye to eye with him on earth, as they do now in the clearer light of heaven.

From Boston, the head-waters of the Narragansett Bay are reached after a pleasant ride of only little more than an hour. There are some forests through which the train shoots, and we tried to people them with Indians—with the genuine savage who so disturbed the quiet of our fathers, and who so severely taxed, but never exhausted, the peace-making resources of Roger Williams. But there was not half a chance for such a dream. Scarcely had we brought before our mind's eye a sage-looking Canonicus, or a stalwart Miantonomo, when the engine screamed its obtrusive alarm, or the conductor shouted the name of some town or village. On reaching the Providence depot, the first person who attracted our attention was as pure a specimen of the natives of the American forest as these degenerate times can produce. She was sitting behind a bench covered with trinkets. A genuine Narragansett! we exclaimed mentally ; perhaps a kindred of some devoted friend of Roger Williams. But on inquiry she proved to be a fresh importation from Canada ! We turned away in disgust, and began our inquiries, with better success, as the reader will see, for a relative of Williams himself.

Provided with a letter of introduction to the courteous Register of Brown University, the Rev. William Douglas, we were introduced by him to the librarian, Mr. R. A. Guild. This last-named gentleman has given special attention to the history of Roger Williams, and is editing, in connection with other literary men, the republication, by the Narragansett Club, of all his works. We found in him a cordial and well-qualified adviser in the prosecution of our inquiries after historic localities. Through a courteous note from him we were soon enjoying the privilege of an interview with Stephen Randall, Esq., a descendant of Roger Williams, whose attention, for many years, has been directed to securing from his fellow-citizens becoming respect to the memory of Roger Williams in the form of a monument. An exceedingly pleasant and instructive conversation on the subject occupied our attention, the gift of several valuable documents in reference to Williams which we had not before seen, and an engagement to accompany us the next day to the Williams localities, were some of the gratifying results of our visit.

Punctual to his engagement, Mr. Randall

met us the next morning. From a point near
the Providence and Boston depot we walked
along Canal-street, and arrived in a few moments at a pump, on the left hand, near the
tide-water. "You may see," remarked Mr.
Randall pleasantly, while pumping, "how you
like water from the Roger Williams spring."
It affords a refreshing supply of pure water in
one of the city thoroughfares of travel. The
spring with which this well is connected by a
pipe is situated a few rods from it up the western side of Prospect Hill. We walked through
a narrow public way to the rear of number 242,
west side of North Main-street. For many
years, until the summer of 1870, the spring was
in the back-yard of this brick dwelling-house.
The city then, to widen the street, moved the
house back, so that the spring is now some-
where near the middle of the cellar. Roger
Williams, when paddling his canoe in search of
a resting-place, shot out of the mouth of the
Seekonk river into what is now the harbor,
rounded Fox Point and ascended "Providence
river," (a narrow upper arm of the Narragansett Bay,) and sailed along its eastern shore, no
doubt then well covered with forests, until he

espied this spring gushing out from the side of the hill. Here he ended his voyage, and built his cabin. A road was laid out above the spring along the whole western declivity of the hill, called King-street, now North Main-street. Six-acre lots were set off on the eastern side of this road, and, of course, extending up the hill ; being narrow, they in fact extended to its top. We then crossed the present street from the spring, and, passing up a lane which opened into the rear of number 233, we stood over the cellar of the Roger Williams house. It stood, as did other early houses, eighty feet from the street. Mr. Randall had often played about it in his boyhood, when Mr. Williams' foot-prints were still there, and the spring below bubbled up into a cask set in the ground for public con-venience. The location commands a wide and varied view. To Williams it was an impressive view of forest-covered hills, green meadows, and a quiet sheet of water. Now we look down from it upon a busy, populous city.

Still further up the .hill, among the trees of his orchard, was the family burial-ground. We reached it by crossing what is now Benefit-street, passing into the rear of number 109, the house of Sullivan Dorr, Esq., through the yard, and, by permission, into the stable, up into its hay-loft, and out of a rear door to the sharply-ascending hill. The grave of Roger Williams is a few feet from the door. It is covered by a finished cap of a heavy stone pillar. The cap was, we suppose, rejected for some reason by the builders, and was taken and placed here as an imperishable index of the place where for nearly two hundred years slept the dust of the apostle of religious liberty.

Mr. Randall remarked that he had been told by the aged people of his boyhood that this was the Roger Williams grave. The tradition concerning it is clear and satisfactory. It once had a head-stone, but traces of it had disappeared, and the place had fallen into general neglect until March, 1860. At that time, under the promptings of Mr. Randall, competent and responsible persons opened the grave. The dust— for that was all that remained of the mortal body of Roger Williams—was carefully and reverently gathered and deposited in an urn, and the urn placed in Mr. Randall's family tomb until further disposition may be made of it. The grave of Mrs. Williams was also examined, and a lock of braided hair was all that indicated where she lay.

A singular incident was discovered on uncovering the bottom of Mr. Williams' grave. The root of an apple-tree had turned out of its way to enter it at the head. Following the position of the body to the thighs, it divided and followed each leg to the feet, tender fibers shooting out in various directions. By nature's promptings it had sought and taken up the chemical deposits of the body, and turned them into blossoms and fruit. So do the virtues of the good bear fruit after their memory among men has perished.

Before parting, Mr. Randall introduced us to the holder of a watch owned and carried by Roger Williams. Its style is of course exceedingly antique. It is a silver Dutch bull's eye, made in Rotterdam, with an enchasing on its 'open silver face of Hector taking leave of his family. It was plainly a first-class article in its day, and is even now a good time-keeper, giving good assurance of running well another two hundred years. It has a curious device by which the day of the month is indicated upon its face. The machinery by which this is done is wound up by the turns of the key which winds its other parts. The date, 1653, is barely discernible. Williams was at this period the guest of Sir Henry Vane, or at least frequently at his mansion, and his intimate friend. He was at the same time, the reader will recollect, in friendly relations with Milton, Cromwell, and Hugh Peters. It may have been to Williams the treasured memento of one of these historic men.

Mr. Randall carries in his pocket a memento scarcely less valuable than the watch. It is a pocket-compass owned by Williams. Besides its needle and points, it has a sun-dial so adjusted that it can be made to throw its shadow upon the hours cut into the brass rim inside of the case. The whole is very portable and artistically finished. We naturally associated it with his "steering" through the woods from Salem to the Narragansett country.

The root which so curiously marked in the grave of Williams the outlines of his bones was the next object of our examination and study. It seemed to us nature's reverent effort to perpetuate the memory of the good man's earthly resting place.

From viewing these localities and curious things we turned toward Whatcheer, or Slate

Rock, the spot on the Seekonk river where Williams landed after being hailed in a friendly manner by the Indians. We present a good fancy sketch of the scene. It is a copy of the device upon the official seal of the city of Providence. The locality may be found by following South Main-street to Power-street, and then going east to the river. Slate Rock is a small affair now, time and curious fingers having carried a large portion of it away. The bank rises abruptly here from the river ; the land in the immediate vicinity, which has hitherto been unoccupied, affords good house lots, and is being rapidly covered. The Rock and this land bear much the same relation to each other as the Forefather's Rock at Plymouth bears to Cole's Hill on the adjacent bank which is graded and kept as a public park, and so ought the other to be ; it would afford a pleasant resort from the more crowded portions of the city, and its moral influence, connecting, as it must, with the memory of the Founder of the State, would be excellent.

It only remains for us to notice recent efforts to erect a suitable monument to the memory of Williams. Many attempts have been made

18

from time to time, and failed. The State not long since atoned in some degree for these failures by appropriating twenty thousand dollars for a statue of Williams, to be placed in the Capitol at Washington. It has been executed by a young artist of great promise, Franklin Simmons, of Providence, and, at the time of our writing, awaits the ceremony of its erection to a place by the side of the historic men of the nation. We present the reader with a picture of it from a photograph by Coleman & Remington, Providence.*

The monumental enterprise took definite form in 1860 by the promptings of our friend, Stephen Randall. An association was formed under an act of incorporation, with the venerable Francis Wayland as its president. The breaking out of the Rebellion, and disagreement concerning the plans for the proposed monument, caused a pause in its operations until 1867. Mr. Randall again came to the rescue, and put its operations on such a footing that ultimate success is certain. His generous gift to its fund gave them spirit and form. A plan of a monument has been definitely determined.

* See Frontispiece.

A picture of it is presented to our readers. It is to be not less than one hundred and seventy feet high. The material of the outer wall is to be granite. Provision is made in the plan for statues and historical inscriptions. The site is also determined. It is to be between Halsey and Angell streets, and within three hundred feet of Prospect-street. This will place it on the top of Prospect Hill, and on the upper part of Roger Williams' "plantation," or six-acre lot. It is to cost not less than $75,000. The site is two hundred feet above tide-water, so that the range of view must be grand and varied. During the Revolution a beacon fire elevated upon a mast from the top of Prospect Hill was seen in Cambridge, Massachusetts, and New London, Connecticut. The monument of Roger Williams will yet greet that of Bunker Hill, and the same setting sun will "linger and play upon the summit" of both.

BOOKS

PUBLISHED BY CARLTON & LANAHAN,

805 Broadway, New York.

Little Songs for Little Readers.

With numerous Illustrations.   Wide 16mo.

This book of songs is just what the little folks in our Sunday schools and families have long wanted.

Ministry of Life.

Five Illustrations.   Wide 16mo.

gilt
Morocco and full calf, gilt

The Christian Maiden.

Memorials of Miss Eliza Hessel.   Wide 16mo.

Muslin, gilt edges
Morocco, gilt edges

A perfect gem.

My Sister Margaret.

Four Illustrations.   Wide 16mo.

gilt
Morocco and full calf

The best temperance book in print.

Pilgrim's Progress.

With numerous Illustrations.   **12mo.**

imitation morocco, gilt

The Object of Life.

A Narrative Illustrating the Insufficiency of the World and the Sufficiency of Christ.   With four Illustrations. Wide 16mo.

full calf, gilt

BOOKS FOR SUNDAY-SCHOOLS.

805 Broadway, New York.

FILIAL DUTY
Recommended and Enforced, by a variety of Instructive and Amusing Narratives of Children who have been Remarkable for Affection to their Parents; also, an Account of some Striking Instances of Children who have been guilty of Cruel and Unnatural Conduct to their Parents. Five Illustrations. 18mo.

SOUTH SEA MISSIONS.
Conversations on the South Sea Missions. By the Author of "Conversations on the Life of Carey." Illustrated. Two volumes, 18mo.

THE LIFE OF DAVID.
By Rev. DANIEL SMITH. 18mo.

IDLE DICK AND THE POOR WATCHMAKER.
Originally written in French, by Rev. CÆSAR MALAN, of Geneva. With Illustrations. 18mo.

THE FEATHER AND SONG BIRD.
Illustrated. 18mo.

THE MIRACLES OF CHRIST:
With Explanatory Observations, and Illustrations from Modern Travels. Intended for the Young. Six Illustrations. 18mo.

THE FLY AND HONEY BEE.
Illustrated. 18mo.

THE NEST AND EGG.
Illustrated. 18mo.

SCRIPTURE CHARACTERS:
Letters on the Distinguishing Excellences of Remarkable Scripture Personages. By Rev. ROBERT HUSTON. 18mo.

THE ANIMALCULE AND GALL INSECT.
Illustrated. 18mo.

THE FORTY-TWO CHILDREN AT MT. BETHEL.
By a Sabbath-School Teacher. 18mo

THE ANT AND SPIDER.
Illustrated. 18mo.

BOOKS FOR SUNDAY-SCHOOLS.
805 Broadway, New York.

CONVERSATIONS ON PALESTINE.
Conversations on the Geography, Natural History, etc., of Palestine. By IMOGEN MERCEIN. Illustrated. 18mo.

THE LIFE OF SAMSON.
By Rev. DANIEL SMITH. 18mo.

MORAL FABLES AND PARABLES.
By INGRAM COBBIN, M. A. Illustrated. 18mo.

STORIES FROM THE HISTORY OF SCOTLAND.
By Rev. ALEXANDER STEWART, a Minister of that Country 18mo.

MATERNAL INSTRUCTIONS;
Or, The History of Mrs. Murray and her Children. By WILLIAM M'GAVIN, ESQ., Author of the Protestant. 18mo.

THE LIFE OF ST. PAUL.
By Rev. DANIEL SMITH. 18mo.

THE DESTRUCTION OF JERUSALEM:
Abridged from the History of the Jewish Wars, by Flavius Josephus. With a Description of Palestine, and brief Sketch of the History of Jerusalem before the War; together with an Epitome of its Modern History, the whole being intended to illustrate the Fulfillment of the Predictions of Moses and the Messiah. By Rev. DANIEL SMITH. 18mo.

WESLEYAN CENTENARY:
A Memorial of the Wesleyan Centenary. Extracted from "The Centenary of Wesleyan Methodism." By THOMAS JACKSON. 18mo.

GRACE KING;
Or, Recollections of Events in the Life and Death of a Pious Youth: with Extracts from her Diary. Published for the benefit of Youth. Three Illustrations. 18mo.

LOVE TO THE SAVIOUR.
By Rev. DANIEL SMITH. 18mo.

THE LIFE OF ST. PETER.
By Rev. DANIEL SMITH. 18mo.

BOOKS FOR SUNDAY-SCHOOLS.
805 Broadway, New York.

NOTICES OF FUH CHAU,
And the other Open Ports of China: with Reference to Mission ary Operations. With Illustrations. 18mo.

THE BIBLE SCHOLAR'S MANUAL:
Embracing a General Account of the Books and Writers of the Old andNew Testaments, the Geography and History of Pales- tine, the History and Customs of the Jews, etc. For Bible Classes and General Reading. By Rev. B. K. PEIRCE. 18mo

THE INDIAN ARCHIPELAGO:
Its Manners, Arts, Languages, Religions, and Institutions By Rev. JAMES RAWSON, A.M. With Illustrations. Two vol- umes, 18mo.

WILLIAM;
Or, The Converted Romanist. Translated from the French. 18mo.

THE LIFE OF CYRUS.
18mo.

THE DAWN OF MODERN CIVILIZATION;
Or, Sketches of the Social Condition of Europe from the Twelfth to the Sixteenth Century. 18mo.

THE FISHERMAN'S SON.
Two Illustrations. 18mo.

MAGIC,
Pretended Miracles, and Remarkable Natural Phenomena. Illustrated. 18mo.

ANGEL WHISPERS;
Or, The Story of Thomas and Edward. Two Illustrations. 18mo.

HISTORY OF NELLY VANNER.
Written expressly for Children. By JOHN CURWEN. 18mo.

PRAISE AND BLAME.
By Rev. CHARLES WILLIAMS, Author of "Facts, not Fables." With Illustrations. 18mo.

2

BOOKS FOR SUNDAY-SCHOOLS.

805 Broadway, New York.

THE EARLY DEAD:

Containing Brief Memoirs of Sunday-School Children. Three volumes, 18mo.

HOSTETLER;

Or, The Mennonite Boy converted. A true Narrative. By a Methodist Preacher. Two Illustrations. 18mo.

MOUNTAINS OF THE BIBLE.

Conversations on the Mountains of the Bible, and the Scenes and Circumstances connected with them in Holy Writ. Supplementary to the "Mountains of the Pentateuch." By E. M. B Four Illustrations. 18mo.

A MISSIONARY NARRATIVE

Of the Triumphs of Grace, as seen in the Conversion of Kaffirs, Hottentots, Fingoes, and other natives of South Africa. By SAMUEL YOUNG, twelve years a Missionary in that Country. 18mo.

JULIANA OAKLEY.

A Tale. By MRS. SHERWOOD, Author of "Little Henry and his Bearer." Two Illustrations. 18mo.

ERMINA:

The Second Part of Juliana Oakley. By MRS. SHERWOOD. Five Illustrations. 18mo.

THE DAIRYMAN'S DAUGHTER:

An Authentic Narrative. By Rev. LEGH RICHMOND. A new edition, comprising much additional matter. 18mo.

LITTLE JANE;

Or, The Young Cottager; The Negro Servant; and other Authentic Narratives. By Rev. LEGH RICHMOND. With Illustrations. 18mo.

LIFE OF REV. LEGH RICHMOND,

Author of the "Dairyman's Daughter," "Young Cottager," etc. By STEPHEN B. WICKENS. 18mo.

SCENES IN THE WILDERNESS:

An Authentic Narrative of the Labors and Sufferings of the Moravian Missionaries among the North American Indians By Rev. WILLIAM M. WILLETT. 18mo.

BOOKS FOR SUNDAY-SCHOOLS.

805 Broadway, New York.

LECTURES TO CHILDREN.
By the Assistant Editor of the "Christian Advocate and Journal," etc. Illustrated. 18mo.

LIFE OF LADY FALKLAND.
The Grace of God Manifested in the Life and Death of Lady Letice Viscountess Falkland. 18mo.

THE RECOLLECTIONS OF A MINISTER;
Or, Sketches drawn from Life and Character. By Rev. J. T. BARR. 18mo.

CHOICE PLEASURES FOR YOUTH:
Recommended in a Series of Letters from a Father to his Son. 18mo.

MEMOIR OF HANNAH MORE:
With brief Notices of her Works, Cotemporaries, etc. By S. G. ARNOLD. 18mo.

THEOBALD, THE IRON HEARTED;
Or, Love to Enemies. From the French of Rev. CÆSAR MALAN. 18mo.

THE DAY-LAMP OF LIFE.
Two Illustrations. 18mo.

THE LIFE OF ESTHER.
By Rev. DANIEL SMITH. 18mo.

THE THEOLOGICAL COMPEND:
Containing a System of Divinity, or a brief View of the Evidences, Doctrines, Morals, and Institutions of Christianity Designed for the benefit of Families, Bible Classes, and Sunday Schools. By AMOS BINNEY. 18mo.

LIFE OF JOHN THE BAPTIST.
By Rev. DANIEL SMITH. 18mo.

THE LIFE OF JONAH.
By Rev. DANIEL SMITH. Two Illustrations. 18mo.

THE LIFE OF ABRAHAM.
By Rev. DANIEL SMITH. 18mo.

BOOKS FOR SUNDAY-SCHOOLS.

805 Broadway, New York.

THE YOUNG MINER:
A Memoir of John Lean, Jun., of Camborne, in the County of Cornwall. By JOHN BUSTARD. 18mo.

THANET SUNDAY-SCHOOL TEACHER.
Mildred, the Thanet S. School Teacher. By JOHN BUSTARD. 18mo.

OLD HUMPHREY'S OBSERVATIONS.
Selections from Old Humphrey's Observations and Addresses Six Illustrations. 18mo.

INTERESTING STORIES
For the Entertainment and Instruction of Young Readers. Illustrated. Two volumes, 18mo.

ELLEN AND SOPHIA;
Or, The Broken Hyacinth. By MRS. SHERWOOD, Author of "Little Henry and his Bearer." Three Illustrations. 18mo.

FARMER GOODALL AND HIS FRIEND.
By the Author of "The Last Day of the Week." With Illustrations. 18mo.

JANE AND HER TEACHER.
A Simple Story. 18mo.

THE MOUNTAIN AND VALLEY.
Two Illustrations. 18mo.

PROCRASTINATION;
Or, Maria Louisa Winslow. By MRS. H. M. PICKARD. 18mo.

CHRISTIAN PEACE;
Or, The Third Fruit of the Spirit. Illustrated by Scenes from Real Life. 18mo.

THE CAVES OF THE EARTH:
Their Natural History, Features, and Incidents. 18mo.

THE BLIND MAN'S SON;
Or, The Poor Student successfully struggling to overcome Adversity and Misfortune. Two Illustrations. 18mo.

3

BOOKS FOR SUNDAY-SCHOOLS.

805 Broadway, New York.

THE CONVERTED JEWESS:

A Memoir of Maria ——. 18mo.,

THE MISSIONARY TEACHER:

A Memoir of Cyrus Shepard, embracing a Brief Sketch of the Early History of the Oregon Mission. By Rev. Z. A. MUDGE. Seven Illustrations. 18mo.

BE GOOD:

An Important Precept illustrated in Ralph's Account of a Visit to the Country. Four Illustrations. 18mo.

HADASSAH;

Or, The Adopted Child. Two Illustrations. 18mo.

THE LIVES OF THE CÆSARS.

For Week-day Reading. Six Illustrations. 18mo.

THE LIFE OF MOHAMMED.

Three Illustrations. 18mo.

THE HIGHLAND GLEN;

Or, Plenty and Famine. Two Illustrations. 18mo.

PARTING PRECEPTS

To a Female Sunday Scholar, on her Advantages and Responsibilities. By Mrs. J. BAKEWELL. 18mo.

NEDDY WALTER;

Or, The Wilderness made to Bloom. Two Illustrations. 18mo.

HARRIET GREY;

Or, The Selfish Girl cured. 18mo.

CUBA.

By Rev. JAMES RAWSON, A. M. Illustrated. 18mo.

THE DEVOUT SOLDIER:

A Memoir of Major General Burn, of the Royal Marines. By Rev. DANIEL WISE, Author of "The Macgregor Family," etc. Two Illustrations. 18mo.

1

BOOKS FOR SUNDAY-SCHOOLS.

805 Broadway, New York.

MISSIONS IN WESTERN AFRICA.
Including Mr. Freeman's Visit to Ashantee. Four Illustrations. 18mo.

AN ESSAY ON SECRET PRAYER,
As the the Duty and Privilege of Christians. By Joseph Entwisle, Minister of the Gospel. 18mo.

JUVENILE TEMPERANCE MANUAL,
And Facts for the People. By D. Goheen, Columbia, Pa. 18mo.

SCRIPTURE PROPHECY.
Fulfillment of Scripture Prophecy, as Exhibited in Ancient History and Modern Travels. By Stephen B. Wickens. Three Illustrations. 18mo.

LIFE OF THE APOSTLE JOHN.
By Rev. Daniel Smith. 18mo.

HISTORY OF THE PATRIARCH JACOB.
By Rev. Daniel Smith. Five Illustrations. 18mo.

THE LIFE OF HEZEKIAH.
By Rev. Daniel Smith. 18mo.

THE LIFE OF JOSHUA.
By Rev. Daniel Smith. Three Illustrations. 18mo.

DEAF AND DUMB.
Recollections of the Deaf and Dumb. 18mo.

THE LIFE OF ELIJAH.
By Rev. Daniel Smith. Five Illustrations. 18mo.

THE WATERLOO SOLDIER.
Three Illustrations. 18mo.

SUPERSTITIONS OF BENGAL:
Anecdotes of the Superstitions of Bengal, for Young Persons. By Robert Newstead, Author of "Ideas for Infants." 18mo.

5

BOOKS FOR SUNDAY-SCHOOLS.

805 Broadway, New York.

STORY OF ANNA THE PROPHETESS.
By a Sabbath-School Teacher. 18mo.

STORY OF ANANIAS AND SAPPHIRA.
By WILLIAM A. ALCOTT. 18mo.

THE JEW AMONG ALL NATIONS.
Eight Illustrations. 18mo.

THE KINGDOM OF HEAVEN
Among Children; or, Twenty-five Narratives of a Religious Awakening in a School in Pomerania. From the German, by CHARLOTTE CLARKE. 18mo.

MOUNTAINS OF THE PENTATEUCH.
Conversations on the Mountains of the Pentateuch, and the Scenes and Circumstances connected with them in Holy Writ. 18mo.

LIFE OF JOHN BUNYAN,
Author of the Pilgrim's Progress. By STEPHEN B. WICKENS. Six Illustrations. 18mo.

THE TWO DOVES:
Or, Memoirs of Margaret and Anna Dove, late of Leeds, England. By PETER M'OWAN. 18mo.

THE MOTHERLESS FAMILY.
Two Illustrations. 18mo.

THOMAS HAWKEY TREFFRY:
) Parental Portraiture of Thomas Hawkey Treffry, who died at Falmouth, April 19, 1821, aged eighteen years. By Rev RICHARD TREFFRY. 18mo.

UNCLE WILLIAM AND HIS NEPHEWS.
Nine Illustrations. 18mo.

MY GRANDFATHER GREGORY.
With Illustrations. 18mo.

THE FLOWER AND FRUIT.
Illustrated. 18mo.

THE SEED AND GRASS.
Illustrated. 18mo.

BOOKS FOR SUNDAY-SCHOOLS.

805 Broadway, New York.

LIFE OF REV. RICHARD WATSON,
Author of Theological Institutes, Dictionary, Exposition of the Gospels, etc. By STEPHEN B. WICKENS. 18mo.

SERIOUS ADVICE
From a Father to his Children. Recommended to Parents, Guardians, Governors of Seminaries, and to Teachers of Sunday Schools. By CHARLES ATMORE. 18mo.

A VOICE FROM THE SABBATH SCHOOL:
A brief Memoir of Emily Andrews. By Rev. DANIEL SMITH. 18mo.

LITTLE JAMES;
Or, The Story of a Good Boy's Life and Death. John Reinhard Hedinguer; or, the Faithful Chaplain : being an Account of an extraordinarily Pious and Devoted Minister of Christ. 18mo.

MEMOIR OF ELIZABETH JONES,
A Little Indian Girl, who lived at the River-Credit Mission, Upper Canada. Three Illustrations. 18mo.

JERUSALEM AND THE TEMPLE.
Rebuilding of Jerusalem and the Temple; or, The Lives of Ezra and Nehemiah. By Rev. DANIEL SMITH. 18mo.

THE TRAVELER;
Or, A Description of Various Wonders in Nature and Art. Illustrated. 18mo.

MEMOIRS OF JOHN FREDERIC OBERLIN,
Pastor of Waldbach, in the Ban De La Roche. 18mo.

THE LIFE OF GEORGE WASHINGTON,
First President of the United States. By S. G. ARNOLD, Author of "Memoirs of Hannah More." Three Illustrations. 18mo.

THE LIFE OF DANIEL.
By Rev. DANIEL SMITH. Two Illustrations. 18mo.

THE LIFE OF MOSES.
By Rev. DANIEL SMITH. Illustrated. 18mo.